I0587676

7 DAYS IN HELL

A COLLECTION OF CHILLING SHORT STORIES

KEVIN M. MOEHRING

The stories told in this collection are strictly fictional and are totally the product of the warped mind of the author. While the names used are real, the characters themselves are entirely made up.

All rights belong to the author.

Copyright 2019

ISBN 978-1-7321567-2-2

"Lots of people want to ride with you in the limo, but what you want is someone who will take the bus with you when the limo breaks down."

--Oprah Winfrey

"We come from homes far from perfect, so you end up almost parent and sibling to your friends – your own chosen family. There's nothing like a really loyal, dependable, good friend, Nothing."

--Jennifer Aniston

"A true friend is someone who thinks that you are a good egg even though he knows you are slightly cracked."

--Bernard Meltzer

FORWARD

Let me start by saying that this project was the most fun I have had since I started my writing journey a few years ago. I had been pondering the idea of a short story collection for some time before actually deciding to go through with it. 7 Days in Hell is my take on some of the classic horror stories and some twisted offerings of my own.

I am lucky enough to have a really close group of friends who mean the world to me. We are all vastly different in our own way, but similar in the ways that matter. When I want to relax and have a good time, it's these friends that I turn to. When life gets stressful, it's these friends that I lean on. I like to think that I provide the same for them, but I'm not sure I could give them the same amount of love, inspiration and support that they have given me over the years.

You might notice that each story in this collection revolves around a single main character. These characters are named for a member of our group, who graciously allowed me to use their names in this work. Parts of each of their story are things that only the two of us will understand, an Easter egg hidden within the plot. Not everything about the characters are identical to my friends, but it was enjoyable to have a face to match up with the names while writing.

You might also notice that one name appears in all the stories. Stephen King would call this person my IR or intended reader. I call her my best friend and my wife. When I started writing and it was merely a hobby, she was the first person I shared my work with. She pushed me and supported me, not just in my writing, but in my life.

This book is a thank you to all my friends, not just the ones who I have immortalized by killing in these stories. I am who I am because of my friends, I am just thankful that I am smart enough to see it. I raise my glass to Jeff who was the best man at my wedding, Susan my Nashville band mate, Kyle my Mardi Gras partner in crime. And to Jessica, the newest member of the group who fit in from day one, Jamie, my brother from another mother, Jeannie the den mother and party hostess extraordinaire and

Shannon the wine drinking calm one of the group. Most importantly, hats off to Robyn. You take my crazy life in stride and put me in my place when I need it. I love you all.

A LONG SLEEP

KYLE'S STORY

7 Days in Hell

1

There are dozens of things that could cause a person insomnia, and ten times that many possible remedies. Some doctors say the disorder is brought on by stress or by a person's diet. Kyle knew exactly what brought on his sleeping disorder. He has failed to sleep more than two or three hours at a time ever since he divorced from his ex-wife. Society is quick to point out the damages done to a child of divorce, and rightly so, but there is rarely any mention of the struggles the husband or wife may have. Most times, the adults had struggled and worked for years to build the family, only to have it dismantled with a simple signature on a court document. Some people have a difficult time adjusting to the new home dynamic, especially those who have become accustomed to the sights and sound of having small children in the home. Kyle is one of these people.

He still gets regular visitation with his kids, and on those nights, he sleeps like a baby. The comfort of knowing he is only a few feet from them puts his mind at ease. It's the nights when the kids are with their mother that gives him the trouble. His insomnia had begun as simple nightmares. Dreams that would wake him up in the middle of the night in a cold sweat. As the months wore on, the fear of waking up every night in a panic forced him to forgo trying to sleep at all. On the rare occasion that he did try to sleep, he would spend countless hours staring up at the ceiling, listening to the ticking of the clock on the wall.

A body needs at least six hours of sleep a night according to the experts, but on the weekends when his kids were away, Kyle was lucky to get six hours of sleep total. He was able to function alright, but his body was beginning to show the signs of exhaustion. He would do anything for his children, but he was also desperate to find a solution to his problem. He tried every sleep doctor in the area. Some tried to diagnose him with sleep apnea, but the overnight tests proved that was not a viable cause. He remembers telling one doctor that it is hard to have sleep apnea when he can't fall asleep to begin with. He quickly gave up on the medical forms of relief and began trying the dozens of cures he found online.

The most common home remedy was exercise. The theory behind it being that if you worked out strenuously before trying to sleep, your body would want to shut down to recover. Kyle tried this for several weekends and the only thing he managed to get was sore muscles. Next, he tried the warm milk theory. Several online sources cited this as being a sure-fire way to way to fall asleep. If it worked for babies, why shouldn't it work for adults? It was only after trying this that Kyle realized he didn't really like warm milk, and neither did his body. He got less sleep than normal thanks to the extra time he was forced to sit on the toilet.

The only real thing that seemed to work for him was alcohol. The online sources said that drinking a glass of wine before bed would help with relieving the stresses from the day. The problem with this is that Kyle can't stand wine. He much prefers to drink beer, but not all beer. He likes the fancy beer with long names that don't make any sense, like summer solstice lager or mountain river IPA. Craft beer and microbrews are his drinks of choice. These beers tend to be a little stronger than the domestic varieties, meaning it takes less of them to get a person drunk. These beers are also the reason that Kyle has now been kicked out of the second bar of the night and is trying to find his car in a drunken stupor.

In his more than thirty-five years on this planet, Kyle had never been kicked out of a single bar. That was before the insomnia led him to begin drinking around noon and still be pouring them back as midnight approached. All he wants to do is get himself to the point where he passes out and gets a restful sleep. Earlier this evening, a game of bar trivia got a little overheated when Kyle decided to argue with the DJ who was asking the questions. He did not agree with the fact that the Vatican was indeed a country, Kyle believing vehemently that it is identified as a city-state. After a few seconds of shouting and name calling, Kyle was shown the door by Robyn, the curly haired bartender. She was polite about asking him to leave but he was made well aware that he was not welcomed back for trivia in the future.

As he strolled down the sidewalk, he knew he had not had enough alcohol to make him sleep, so he looked for his next drinking establishment. He had never been inside The Honey Hole, even though he had seen it numerous times. The strip club was dark when he entered and much to his chagrin, only sold domestic beer. As he began to drink, his eyes darted around the room to the hopeless men, each looking more and more pathetic as they toss money at women who looked like they needed a cheeseburger more than a few dollars. He was on his fourth beer when the most amazing woman he had ever seen came onto the stage in front of him. She was tall and athletically built with well-toned and tan legs. Her thong panties rode high on her hips and matched the lacy bra that covered very little of the blonde's breasts. Kyle was instantly smitten.

The woman danced her two songs and Kyle threw as much cash in her direction as he could. He didn't care that he had now become one of the desperate men sitting on the side of the stage throwing money at this woman just to see her take her clothes off. She was a master of manipulation, making the men around the stage feel like she was dancing for only them. The way she would smile at him and give him a playful little wink, made Kyle feel like the goddess of a woman was seriously into him. He didn't frequent strip clubs and didn't know the tricks the dancers used to maximize the amount of money you threw at them. Between the galloons of alcohol he had consumed, and the complete exhaustion he was feeling, Kyle couldn't hold back the feeling any longer.

As Chesty Bazooms, the awful stage name for the stunning blonde, made her way off the stage, Kyle decided to act. He walked directly to the woman, who seemed a bit in shock to see him confront her. He wasted no time and went straight in, planting a huge kiss on the face of the dancer, allowing his hands to grab at her backside as he did. He didn't get the desired response from neither Chesty Bazooms or the security staff at The Honey Hole. For a man who had never been thrown out of a bar before, this second time was iconic. The dancer brought her knee up and connected with a strong blow to his crotch. As Kyle reeled back, his arms were caught by two giant security guys. They wasted no time in picking up the drunk man and tossing him onto the sidewalk. Kyle landed hard on the concrete, his face taking the brunt of the impact.

Crushed by the lack of interest from the dancer and defeated to the point where he wanted to cry, Kyle decided it was time to go home. The only problem with that was he was far more intoxicated than he had thought. When the cool night air hit his face, the world began to spin. He looked around the unfamiliar landscape, searching for a building or façade that would help him remember where he parked his car. Everything looked different in the dark than it did when he first got here about twelve hours ago. He is beginning to regret his decision to travel north about thirty miles from his home. He made the trip hoping to avoid seeing people he knew. When you're on a mission to get drunk enough to pass out, the last thing you want to see is people you might know.

A highly intoxicated voice in his head tells him that he could just walk home, it would be a straight shot down interstate seventy-five. The drunk part of his mind tries to convince him he could be in his bed in less than three hours if he did so. Luckily, right now, Kyle can't even figure out how to get to the interstate. As he stumbles aimlessly down the street, he begins to look for some place where he can rest for a while. He has been drinking for over twelve hours and he just needs to sit down and allow his body to sober up slightly. He's confident that this will allow him to think more clearly, find his car and make his way home. He has no idea what is around in the area, or even what would still be open at this late hour.

After circling the block, his eyes are drawn to the warm fluorescent lights outside a small catholic church. There is no doubt that the doors to the church will be open and at this time of night, he would likely be the only person in the building. Kyle would go to church regularly when he was still married, but they were not catholic. The whole sitting, standing and kneeling routine seemed like an exercise in futility to him. He didn't understand the point. As he opens the large wooden doors of the church, the strong smell of incense overwhelms him. He's careful not to let the heavy door slam behind him, not wanting to draw any unneeded attention his way if there happened to be someone inside the building.

His footsteps echo through the cavernous space. He eyes are drawn to the sacristy and the altar. The large marble statues seem to look down on him in disgust. This is another reason why Kyle didn't really care for the catholic religion. Between the judgmental eyes on the statues and the intricate paintings on the wall, he always felt like he was being looked down upon, like he wasn't holy enough to be in the place of worship. If the figures knew what he had been doing all day, and why he was thrown out of the strip club, they would probably come to life and shower him with lightning bolts.

The altar seems to be well lit, but only by candlelight. There are dozens of flames, so many that the smoke has cast the area in a light fog. Kyle isn't thinking clearly enough to wonder if churches are lit like this every night or not, so he looks for the darkest corner. He slides down the rear most pew and sits down on the wooden bench. It takes only seconds for his body to begin to relax and the elusive feeling of sleep creeps in. Not wanting to be caught sleeping in the church, he decides to hide himself under the bench. The space is confining, but Kyle is skinny and wiggles under the pew with little effort. Nestled under the bench and hidden from view of anyone who would walk down the center aisle, he falls to sleep without even trying, something that has not happened in months.

2

The sound of chanting wakes Kyle in a panic. He had been sleeping so soundly that when he wakes, he has no idea where he is and practically bangs his head against the bottom of the wooden bench. The sounds and echoes that vibrate around the walls of the church add to his awkward wakening, causing him to nearly scream in surprise. He takes a moment to gather his senses, only vaguely remembering where he fell asleep and why. He looks at his watch and sees that it's only a little past three in the morning. He had only been asleep for less than three hours, but his head feels much clearer than it did earlier. He still has no idea where the chanting is coming from, nor can he make out what is being said. The female voices all speak in unison but if they are saying actual words, then it's a language Kyle has never heard before.

He rolls slowly out from under the bench. The ground he had been laying on was carpeted so it was easy to move without making too much noise. As he brings his body to his knees, allowing his head to peak over the back of the bench in front him, he can see the women who are responsible for waking him up. The dozen or so women stand in a semi-circle on the altar.

The way they are dressed makes him think that he is still asleep and dreaming. Each woman is wearing a dark hood which covers her head and drapes along the length of her shoulder. Other than that, they are all naked. He can only see most of them from behind but there is no mistaking their lack of clothing. The one woman standing in the middle of the altar facing the others, is stunning. She is even more gorgeous than the stripper Kyle fell in love with at first sight. There is something about her face that gives him butterflies whenever he looks at her.

The leader stands in front of the half-circle of women, leading the others in a steady chant of words that don't make sense in English. Her long auburn hair falls loosely below her hood, her hood being the only one that is white. Her stomach is tone and her breasts seem to sit on her chest as if lifted from an invisible bra. To say that Kyle was immediately infatuated with the naked leader would be the understatement of the century. In fact, he was infatuated with all the women. He thinks to himself that maybe he should start going to catholic churches more often, especially if this is what goes on inside late at night.

He still hasn't figured out what the women are doing, but as he continues to watch, a new sound enters the room. The grinding of metal on metal pierces over the chants. From high above the women, a naked male figure begins to be lowered. Kyle looks above the man and sees the system of ropes and pulleys used to lower him to their level. The man looks to be in his early twenties, skinny and balding. Kyle can't help but notice the similarities between the man above the altar and himself. Kyle began losing his hair early in his high school years. If the bullies in school weren't making fun of his lack of hair, they were calling him by the other name they loved to use, Boner. This name was given to for obvious reasons, based solely on his skinny frame and his apparent resemblance to an erect penis.

Watching this man being lowered above the women is sort of an out of body experience, the whole thing playing out in front of him like a live action movie. Kyle watches intently, keeping as much of his body hidden behind the back of the church pew as he can. Suddenly, the chants from the women stop. The silence is eerie. Kyle holds his breath in both fear and panic as to what is about to happen. The metal grinding sound stops as the man in the sky must have reached his final destination. He is tied from both his wrists and ankles, positioned horizontal to the ground and only inches from the top of the white hood of the female leader. The woman doesn't even look up. If she did, she would likely be staring straight into the genitalia of the naked man.

The leader takes two steps forward, looking each of the women in the face as she does so. She begins shouting in single word sentences. The words still make no sense to Kyle. Each word seems to be made up of far too many consonants and not nearly enough vowels. He can see the spit fly from her mouth as she emphasizes each syllable of the hard to pronounce words. His eyes scan the back of each of the women as the leader speaks to them directly. Kyle must have missed something, because when he returns his eyes to the leader, she is now holding a gold dagger. The blade of the knife glistens with the refracted light from the numerous candles scattered around the altar. The handle, which only protrudes from her clinched fist a few inches, is gold and ornately decorated. The tension on the altar is so thick he can feel it all the way in the rear of the church.

Without provocation, the leader reaches up with her dagger and slices the man's chest wide open. She runs the sharp blade from his belly button to his chin, spilling out the man's intestines. The circle of naked women quickly disperses, each woman now carrying a large challise. They use their fancy cups to catch as much of the man's blood as they can. Kyle stares at them in disbelief. It took everything he had to not cry out in shock, but as he watches the women begin to drink the blood from their cups, he can't help himself. He rises to his feet as fast as he can, banging his gangly legs against the wood several times. His movements were so loud that when he looked back at the women as he worked his way to the end of his pew, every face was focused on him.

All the women have blood dripping down their face, but the leader is practically covered in it. They make no effort to move toward him, so Kyle takes that as a sign to increase the speed of his exit. The faster he tells himself to leave the church, the more he stumbles and falls to the ground. As he nears the large wooden door to the outside, he looks back one last time. The black hooded women have not moved a muscle and look like they are blood covered statues on the altar. When he turns back to the door, somehow the woman in the white hood is standing between him and the exit. He hadn't seen her come toward him or felt her presence when he turned his head, but she is there. She is so close to him that Kyle gets a strong whiff of the coppery smell of the now dead man's blood.

He tries to maintain eye contact with the woman, but it's nearly impossible. Her eyes are very dark and seem hollow. He has never seen a woman who looks like this before. His eyes drift downward, to the exposed breasts of the woman. When he does, his glare is met with a strong slap from the leader. She doesn't say anything to him. She simply looks at him, or more precisely, looks through him. She slowly begins closing the short distance between their bodies, getting close enough that he can feel her breath on his neck. In a move not too different from what Kyle did in the strip club, the leader grabs his head and licks the side of his face. Her tongue is hot on his skin, unlike anything he has ever felt before. When the woman uses her free hand to grab his crotch, Kyle can no longer hold back his panic. As much as he wants to appear tough in front of her, his body has other ideas. His bowels let loose of a day's worth of craft beer and sends a golden shower of warm liquid down his legs.

The naked leader only smiles when she feels the liquid touch her skin. She releases her grip on his testicles and brings her hand to her own face. She sticks out her tongue and licks the back of her hand and smiles again. She then takes the same hand and places it on Kyles forehead. The sensation sends his body into convulsions. The heat and electricity of her touch send his senses into overload. His mind and vision go dark as his body stiffens. He falls like a tree to the tiled floor of the church, his head hitting the ground with a loud thud.

3

The pounding in his head is intense. He has regained the use of most of his senses, except for his vision. He blinks several times but can't get rid of the complete darkness. He is vaguely attentive to the numerous hands touching every part of his body. Small hands on his chest, hips and feet. He has no idea what has happened but the last thing he can remember is the leader touching his forehead. When the dark hood is removed from his face, he is relieved, having feared that he had lost his vision from the surge of power the women somehow sent through his body. Squinting has very little effect on shielding his eyes from the brightness of the candles as he is forced to stare directly at the ceiling.

It's difficult for him to move. The bones and muscles have all tensed up to the point where they refuse the commands from his mind. As he begins to relax and get comfortable, his body is being moved without his knowledge. He can feel the ropes pulling at him from several directions, but the walls of the church seem to be spinning. When the swaying stops, Kyle gets the sudden urge to vomit. He can taste it rising into his mouth, but he fights with everything he has and forces the mushy contents of his stomach back to where they belong. When the movement stops, he feels the pressure on his wrists release. His arms have been positioned over his head and are beginning to ache. When he begins to lower them, a voice from behind stops his movement.

"I wouldn't do that!"

Kyle turns and sees the white hooded woman staring at him. The rest of the women are positioned behind her, looking at the new prisoner with anxious eyes. He hadn't felt like he had been elevated when his body stopped moving, but now he looks down on the collection of women from a few feet above. He is standing on the altar. The same altar that the church uses every day during their services. The precarious position allows him to get a better view of his surroundings and the severity of his predicament. The small hands he had felt while waking up, were working feverishly to not only tie him up, but they also stripped him of all the clothes he was wearing. There is an instant irony that flashes through his mind about being naked. Being surrounded by a dozen naked women, would be a dream scenario in almost every situation. This, however, is not a normal situation.

"What do you want? Why can't I lower my arms?" Kyle is not one who would normally beg, but desperate times call for desperate measures.

"That would seal your fate. I don't want you to do that until we are ready. The anticipation is what makes it fun for my girls."

The leader is speaking to him, but the words don't match the motion of her lips. Her lips appear to move much slower than they should to say the words he hears, much like the old Kung-Fu movies that he used to watch on Saturday mornings after the cartoons. It occurs to Kyle that she is probably still uttering the same gibberish that she was chanting earlier, except somehow, he understands it now. He wonders what it was exactly that happened to his brain when she touched his head. On top of the weird way she is talking, he also noticed that she failed to look him in the eyes. She had her eyes focused on a region much lower, towards his crotch. When he looks down to see what she was looking at, he sees why.

The sight of it forces him to begin sobbing. Looking up towards the rafters of the church, where he had seen the pulley system used to lower the first man, Kyle sees that he is in a world of trouble. The women have wrapped a thin wire, either piano wire or strong fishing line, around his testicles and the shaft of his penis. The line was wrapped several times and was so tight that it had already begun to cut its way through the soft skin. The thin ring of pink that surrounds the line lets Kyle know that there is very little slack, and the line is plenty strong enough to severe his man parts if enough tension is applied.

It's hard to see, but he tries to follow the other end of line toward the ceiling. By his best guess, the other end of the line snakes through the pulley and wraps around his hands. The thought terrifies him. If he were to lower his hands, or heaven forbid, try to get down from the altar, he would turn himself into a eunuch. His knees buckle at the thought of losing the parts of his anatomy that he likes the most. This time he can't hold back the urge and begins vomiting. The sound of the regurgitation bellows through the church, as Kyle empties the contents of his stomach all over himself and the marble altar where he stands. The force of this action makes him lower his hands the slightest bit. A body is trained to try to cover the mouth whenever coughing, sneezing or in this case, throwing up. There is only slight pressure on his genitals as the wire digs further into his flesh and a few of the hooded women giggle with excitement. Blood begins to trickle down his leg before dotting the top of the marble surface.

4

The hooded women take turns circling around his naked body. Every time they pass behind him, they give him a whack on his butt with a large wooden paddle, something else that just seemed to appear out of nowhere. Every time the blow comes, Kyle first winces from the sting and then fights to keep his balance. The vomit might as well be oil on top of the marble altar. His feet continually slip and slide over the surface, but he has yet to stumble enough to cause any further damage to his genitals. He has repeatedly tried to plead for mercy. For some reason, it doesn't even appear like the group of women even heard him speak.

One by one the women stop circling him and take up positions lower on the altar. The leader assumes her position at the front once more, with her back to his damaged body. This is the first time that he has taken the time to look at the women closely. He is trying to keep his eyes from darting to their chests, but the large tattoo they each have makes it impossible. Right in the middle of their chest plate, perfectly framed by their breasts, each woman has an identical tattoo of a pentagram. How he had not noticed it earlier is beyond him, but now Kyle can look at nothing else. He doesn't notice that the women all appear to have their eyes closed yet continue to function in a normal manner. The fact that they seem to hover a couple of feet off the ground was lost on him as well until he tried looking at the ground to avert his eyes from their chests.

Fear boils in his body at the realization that these women are far from human. It would help explain several things, mainly how they were able to move around without touching the ground and the blank stare that they all seem to have in the brief moments when they open their eyes. It also ensures that the likelihood of him getting out of this situation is slim. He thinks that he must be dreaming. He is a logical thinker and there is no logical way that these women could be hovering above the ground. He sobs again. His theatrical attempt for pity goes unnoticed by the leader who continues to face the group of women, whom she referred to as her girls.

"This is a special day girls. Our God has smiled down upon us. First, he gave us a sinner and allowed us to drink. He provided us with nourishment so that we can continue to carry on his work." The whole time the leader is speaking, the rest of the women continue to hover above the ground. They nod their heads at the appropriate times with creepy smiles on their faces. "Our God has sent us another sinner. Our God wants us to be well fed. He provides for us a bounty on this night. Together, as a group, we will feast once more."

When she finishes her speech, the group of women begin to move closer toward the altar. Kyle can see them creeping closer and closer. His body has been sweating throughout the entire ordeal, but now sweat drips from everywhere. He tries to look at every woman, looking for one who might have an ounce of sympathy for him. His looks are repeatedly returned with closed eyes and sideways grins from the throng of naked women advancing toward him. He has lost sight of the leader. The woman seems to vanish and reappear at will, something else that Kyle can't quite explain.

When the herd of women stop again, they part in the middle. The leader makes her way through them, carrying a large torch. The flame shoots several feet into the air and is so large that Kyle can feel the heat from it on his bare skin. She walks methodically, without a care in the world. The flames shoot wildly from every direction of the torch, several times seemingly going straight through the women's auburn hair or through her blood-stained skin. Kyle looks at her with astonishment. He tries to kick at her with one foot as she walks along the side of the altar, but all he managed to do was fling up loose pieces of vomit into the air.

"This man entered our sanctuary. He took it upon himself to watch us conduct our most holy act. Now he will feel the power that our God gives us. Now, he belongs to us!"

The woman screams the last word and the rest of the women join in on the triumphant cheering. They hoot, holler and scream as Kyle sobs uncontrollably. The white hooded woman silences the crowd of women with a single snap of her finger. She turns quickly and faces Kyle again, this time, her eyes are open, and he can see the evil they contain. The entire eye is dark, almost black. She throws her free hand into the air. With extra flair and a little too much drama, the woman makes a circular motion with her closed fist before opening it and tossing an invisible substance across the top of the altar. Kyle couldn't see anything come out of the woman's hand, but he instantly got the sensation that the skin on the tops of his feet were on fire. She slowly lowers the torch, which at this point is raging larger than it had at any point. The moment the flame touches the marble, the entirety of the surface erupts into an inferno. Kyle, still trying to keep his hands raised and his balls intact, is helplessly stuck right in the middle

5

"Burn Him!"

"Burn Him!"

"Burn Him!"

The chanting women can barely be heard over the roaring of the flames around him and his own screams. The smell of his own burning flesh begins to rise through his nostrils, but it takes several minutes before he realizes what the smell is. His feet are burning. Whatever invisible thing the woman tossed all over the altar has worked like an accelerant and increased the tenacity of the flames. There is nowhere for him to safely put his feet or even move his body to get away from the unbearable heat.

"Burn Him!"

"Burn Him!"

"Burn Him!"

The chanting becomes louder now as he can feel the skin on the soles of his feet begin to stick to the altar and peel away. He is over six feet tall and the flames rise as high as his thighs. He is quickly getting to the point where he needs to make a decision. He only has two options, and neither is appealing. If he stays put, he will most likely burn to a crisp while these women celebrate. If he were to try and make a leap for it, there is a slight chance that whatever wire they used to secure his genitals would break. It doesn't necessarily mean that he will be free, but at least it would stop him from being burned alive. This second option is the one he is contemplating the most, but it also comes with a severe penalty. If the wire is strong enough to hold, he will have castrated himself and would probably bleed out. Kyle is smart enough to know that an injury that severe would cause him to lose too much blood to survive. He must ponder these choices, knowing he is deciding how he wants to die.

These thoughts go through his mind in fractions of a second. The chaos surrounding him didn't give him ample time to work through each scenario properly before deciding. He's got to act quickly. With what little relaxed thinking he had left, he decided if he were going to make a leap from this altar, he was going to go right after the leader. It's hard to find her through the fire, all the faces begin to look alike when blurred by the pain and flames. When he spots her, he wastes zero time. With his hands held as high in the air as he can get them, he takes two big steps toward her and jumps through the flames.

"Burn Him!"

"Burn Him!"

"Burn"

The last portion of the chant was interrupted when the women see him leap from the burning altar toward their leader. Kyle felt a tug at his crotch, but little more, and he needed to get out of the fire. He could see the dark eyes of the woman as his smoking body flies toward her. When she wasn't there to grab ahold of or soften his fall, he crashes like a rock to the ground. The woman had disappeared, vanished at the very last second. He landed hard on his back. Other than the crashing into the hard floor, the only thing he sensed was the warmth coming from his crotch. When he looks down and sees the blood squirting from the area where his genitals once were, he vomits again. He didn't feel the wire slice right through his man parts. The cut was so fast and swift that the soft skin of his penis offered little resistance.

He closes his eyes, fearing what is coming next. When he opens them again, he glances to one side and sees the same marble statue looking down on him that he saw when he first snuck into the church. He gives the holy figure the middle finger in his mind. His head turns slowly back toward the ceiling, his view now obstructed by the thirteen women looking down on him. They all smile, but there is no real joy in their faces. The darkness of their hollow eyes only show pain. Kyle returns their look with one of his own. His smile is genuine. Yes, he may have been darn near burned to death. Yes, he may have castrated himself and yes, he was going to die. But in the end, he is going to get the one thing he has been seeking. Kyle is going to sleep.

FEEDING TIME

SHANNON'S STORY

7 Days in Hell

1

The night shift at the hospital can be a lonely and boring place. Most of her patients sleep more than usual babies. As the head nurse at the Neonatal Intensive Care unit at the largest hospital in the city, Shannon sees the worst of the worst babies. The ones born addicted to drugs are the most troubling. The parents are oblivious to the dangers they have put their unborn children through, and it makes Shannon furious. When the babies are brought into the world, screaming and shaking, addicted to heroin or crack or whatever dangerous substance the mother was using while pregnant, it's Shannon's job to care for the newborns. Its agonizing work, taxing both her physical status with the long hours, and the mental aspect of dealing with parents who could care less about the outcome of the children they have brought into this cruel world. The job is not without its benefits as well. There is no better feeling than seeing the newborns begin to breathe on their own and eventually add enough weight to leave the intensive care unit.

She is thankful to be leaving the hospital on time this morning. There were no emergencies during her shift, and she has big plans for the rest of the day. She has managed to load her trunk with food for her kids who will be waiting at home for her. Is has been far too long since she has been able to provide them with a meal this substantial and she's eager to see their well-fed faces. As she drives along the highway, going the opposite direction of the rush of morning traffic, she turns the radio up and sings along. She lives her life one day at a time and has no one to care for at home other than the reptiles she calls her kids. The large snakes and lizards that dwell in her basement began as a passion of her oldest child. She was more than happy to pamper to his unique obsession, buying him the first two snakes, even though she has always been fearful of the creatures. Parents will always provide for their kids, no matter what strange thing interests them. For some kids it's sports. For others, it could be music. For Shannon's son, it was collecting snakes. Like most kids do, he lost interest in the creatures and left them in the basement when he went away to college. That meant it was mom's responsibility to feed and care for them, which she has done diligently over the past four years.

She had never been a fan of snakes when she was a little girl. In fact, you could say she had a fear of them. The thought of having several living in her basement, where they were free to move around the room as they wanted, would have terrified her. Now she looks at them as if they were her own kids. She even calls them all by name and treats them as a mother would. She even has her favorites. There are seven large snakes in all, but Lucky, the green Emerald Tree Boa named for her favorite Jennifer Aniston movie, is by far her favorite. Lucky is only four feet long and weighs no more than ten pounds, but the best thing about him is that he likes to curl up on Shannon's shoulder to rest. If Powder, the albino python, was smaller and easier to manage, he would probably be her favorite. She remembers the look on her son's face when she brought Powder home. The cream-colored skin of the tiny snake looked eerie in the darkness of the basement even then. He got his name because his son mentioned how it looked like the snake had taken a bath in powder when she first brought it home. Now that the snake has grown to well over fourteen feet and weighs a couple hundred pounds, Shannon tends to keep her distance from him. He is the one snake that scares her.

Most people would say she was odd for having snakes roaming her basement, but to Shannon they are the only family she has. Her kids are both away at school and other than work and the occasional get together with friends, who have no idea about who Shannon shares her home with, her reptile kids are the only interaction she gets. The animals give her the affection she needs to stay sane, even if they have no idea they are doing it. Many times, when a newborn dies on her shift, Shannon wants nothing more than to go straight home with a bottle of wine and sit in the basement. She talks to the snakes. She doesn't talk to them like the crazy cat lady who we all grew up next to. She knows the snakes will not answer her and she doesn't pretend they do. With a job that can be as stressful as hers, Shannon just needs to talk out loud and work things out. The snakes don't interrupt and listen quietly until she has said what she needed to say.

She drives her SUV robotically, on the same route she has taken for the last seven years, as if today was just another day. She turns her car right and exits the highway. The pang of hunger begins to growl in her stomach. She was supposed to meet her friend Robyn for breakfast this morning, but all she wants to do now is get home and feed her children. She slides her fingers over the keypad on her phone and sends her friend a message saying she can't make it. She uses her typical excuse, that she is on call for the hospital and needs to be ready and available. Robyn is one of her closest friends, but every time they get together, they tend to start drinking and before they know it, they are both drunk. Shannon can't afford to be drunk today. She needs to feed the children. They are counting on her to provide. They have been lethargic in recent days, the sure sign that they need to be fed. The cost of keeping reptiles well-nourished has been challenging, but like any other single mother, Shannon works hard and does what needs to be done to keep the animals healthy.

She was so engrossed in her cell phone and the thoughts of feeding the snakes, that she hadn't noticed the police officer who had pulled his cruiser in behind her. There was only a fraction of a second between the time she saw him behind her, and he lit up the blue and red lights. As she made the turn onto Color Street, only two blocks from her house, she nudged the SUV over to the shoulder. Her heart began racing as the officer made his way to her window. As she peeks at the man walking toward her, she sees him place the palm of his hand on the rear bumper of her car. She holds her breath, fearing the cop has figured out her secret. Shannon is no different than every other driver on the road, when the blue and red lights come on behind you, you begin to hyperventilate. Every driver feels the rumble in their stomach whenever they get pulled over. Shannon has a different feeling. Her car is not like every other car on the road. Her car has two bodies in the back.

2

The officer was casual when he began speaking to her. Shannon thought he would have pulled his gun right away and ordered her out of the vehicle. Instead, he began making small talk. He asked her about her night and once he noticed her name badge from the hospital, started talking about her employment. The entire ordeal began to take on a surreal feeling. The officer even opened her door for her when he asked her to step out so he could show her why he pulled her over. As the two walked toward the back of the car, Shannon couldn't help her eyes from looking into the back window. She had taken very little precaution and the bodies of her two victims were clearly visible. When they turn the corner and the cop points at her rear bumper, Shannon feels a little calmer.

Her friends had begun a fantasy football league and since she had finished in last place, her car was adorned with the frame around her license plate that stated as much. Somehow, this frame had been jarred loose and was now hanging haphazardly, covering more than half of the plate itself. Shannon watched as the officer returned to his cruiser, retrieved a screwdriver, and securely reattached the frame. The process took less than five minutes, but it was the most excruciating five minutes of her life. All the guy had to do was be a little nosey and peek into her rear storage compartment. If he did, he would have seen the two unconscious bodies and life as she knew it would cease to exist. Luckily the cop simply smiled and returned to his own car, none the wiser.

As she gets back into the driver's seat, Shannon says a small prayer, thankful that she was heading home and not to prison. She drives well under the speed limit the remaining two blocks to her house and releases a huge sigh of release when she parks her car around the back of her house. She remains seated, staring in the rearview mirror, in anticipation of the cop following up her driveway. She was more daring in kidnapping her victims, far more daring than she had been in the past. Maybe it was because she has become overly confident in her abilities. Maybe it was the fact that her reptile children need the food so badly. Whatever it was, she vows to be more cautious next time.

The women in her trunk were the typical people she would see in her unit. The mother was addicted to crack cocaine and had delivered her child over the weekend. She never once came to the NICU to see her baby. All the woman seemed to care about was getting out of the hospital and getting her next fix. Her sister, who was the person who brought the mother to the hospital, was hooked on the drug even more. On the rare occasion when the mother would come to visit her newborn, she didn't do it for the reasons a sober mother would. This woman would spend her time at the hospital trying to distract as many members of the staff as she could so her sister could pilfer through the storage bins, taking handfuls of needles and any medication they could find. Shannon had seen drug addicts like these women more often than she liked to admit. On the ladder of human decency, these two girls were below the bottom rung. This is how Shannon was able to justify her actions. She has seen several mothers like this in the past, and rarely would she feel comfortable sending a newborn child home with one. Every time she saw a mother who only cared about getting high, Shannon wanted to feed them to her kids.

She was smart enough to know that she couldn't kidnap every mother who she thought needed to die. There were dozens of them that rolled through the hospital every month. She only took the risk on the worst of the worst, but only after doing enough recognizance that she felt confident the abduction would meet little resistance. It was also important that the women she chose were loners and wouldn't be missed. The last thing Shannon needed was for the families of her victims to start asking questions.

Timing was always critical to the success of her plan. She needed the intended victims to still be at the hospital when her shift ended. Everything today worked out perfectly. On her way to the parking garage, she had seen the druggies looking nervous as they entered the lady's restroom. When Shannon rolled up on the two as they left the hospital, it took very little coaxing to get them into the car. A smile, a wave of a fresh needle and the sight of a baggie full of white powder was all it took. She had convinced the two druggies that she would take them somewhere quiet where they could take their time getting high. They were more than willing to hop in the car. Once they were in the backseat, Shannon showed them a baggie, which the two believed was cocaine. Shannon had mixed up the concoction the night before and while it was not pure cocaine, it would get the girls high enough to make them pass out. She was constantly toying with the combination of drugs she used to subdue her victims, this time, she went a little heavy. Once the drugs took effect the two women passed out almost immediately. Shannon had very little trouble rolling their bodies back to the storage area of her car.

Shannon is not a tiny woman, but even with her curvy frame she struggles a bit to get the two women out of her car. The drugs have not begun to wear off, so the dead weight of the women makes them almost impossible to move. It takes every ounce of strength to get the bodies near the shed in her back yard. The next thing she must do is the one thing she hates most about feeding her reptile babies this way. If she were to throw the two lifeless bodies into the basement, it would be impossible to make sure that all the snakes get fed. Powder is plenty large enough to swallow either of the women by himself. She has made that mistake in the past and has since come up with a solution. It's grotesque and bloody, but it's a solution none the less.

She feels alone and safe in the solitude of her backyard. Her house sits on an over-sized lot and is surrounded on every side by large trees. Her nearest neighbors are about half a mile away so there is no chance that anyone would hear, or more importantly see, what is about to happen. Shannon fills the mouths of her victims with dried leaves and dirt, stuffing the cavity as full as she can get it, before wrapping plastic wrap around their noses and mouths. She has learned that her children are more attentive to the food when it smells and tastes like dirt. The plastic wrap has the added benefit of muffling the screams if either of them were to regain consciousness before they were dead. Plus, Shannon has an odd fetish of wanting to look into the eyes of the victims at the very moment they die.

Confident that she has secured the women on the ground, Shannon heads into the tiny shed. There are several tools she has used over the years, saws, machetes, and even a butcher knife, but none of them produced the desired effect. She has finally found a tool that works perfectly and has used it the last couple of times she brought food home. The long pole hangs on the wall of the shed, the chainsaw on the end has been kept in pristine condition. The man who sold her the instrument in the hardware store assured her that she would be able to stand several feet away and be in no danger of flying debris whenever she was using the chainsaw. Shannon didn't even know they made things like this for trimming tree branches, but the man once again assured her the tool is very effective. Little did the man know that Shannon would be using it to cut humans into bite sized pieces.

3

The sound of the saw is loud, but every time it cuts through the soft flesh of the two women, the sound softens. Having the ability to extend the pole the saw is attached to allows for Shannon to make the necessary cuts without covering herself in blood. It's not that she is squeamish or can't stand the site of blood, she is a nurse after all, but having her body covered in blood would just make things messy. If she were covered in blood, she would need a shower, which would take away from the time she would be able to spend in the basement watching the snakes enjoy their meal. Even though she has done this several times, she still likes to see the faces of the victims as she slices through them. Each face is different, and every victim has a different look when they realize they are moments away from dying. Some may call it odd. Some may even call it sadistic. To Shannon, taking pride in slicing up these women is no different than a mother who slaves over a stove all evening and provides a warm meal for her family.

These women failed to react at all, which Shannon attributes to a judgement in error while mixing the drugs. There is no rhyme or reason to how she dissects the bodies in front of her and after the initial cut or two, Shannon can't stand to look at them any longer. Whenever the blade slices through the stomach and spills the contents onto the concrete driveway, it always causes Shannon to vomit. This time is no exception. The coppery smell of the blood mixing with the putrid aroma from the contents of the women's stomachs forces Shannon to drop the saw and throw up everything in her own stomach into the nearest bush. As she brushes the remaining vomit from her mouth with the sleeve of her shirt, she looks down on her victims. For the first time she feels the slightest bit of remorse.

There is no doubt that these two women had very little to offer society. The fact that one of them had no problem doing drugs while several months pregnant is an offense that should be punishable by death in Shannon's mind. This is just another justification she makes for her murderous actions. The scene on the driveway looks far worse than most emergency rooms the nurse has seen. She uses her foot to kick random limbs, making sure the bodies have been cut into small enough pieces that her children will have no problem digesting them. She remembers that some of the smaller snakes have trouble with the larger portions and takes special care in cutting off the fingers off the women with the chainsaw. She smiles as she looks down at the fingers, knowing that Lucky will probably eat them right out of her hands like he did last time.

Shannon returns the chainsaw to the shed and moves a wheelbarrow near the dismembered bodies. This is the first time that she has noticed how skinny the women were. There is hardly any meat on the bones as she tosses the limbs into the wheelbarrow. There is a real fear that she may need to do this again much sooner than she had hoped. She leaves the fingers laying on the concrete and wheels the bodies near the cellar door at the rear of the house. When she swings open the door, she can see the eyes of Powder glowing from the darkness below. The giant snake is looking up at her, anticipating the meal and waiting for the first bit of meat. Shannon is methodical as she tosses the limbs, trying to spread them out as best as she can. She knows the large iguana will be the quickest to the meal, he is much faster than any of the snakes in the basement. By spreading out where she tosses the pieces, it allows the slower big snakes a chance to get a good meal as well.

The feeding frenzy in the basement puts all the animals on high alert. There is no way that Shannon would attempt to go down there and sit among them while they were fighting for dominance. She takes this time to go through her ritualistic cleaning routing. The first time she fed the children this way, she was amazed at the amount of blood that was left on the concrete pad. She had a drain installed on her driveway not long after. It allows her to hose down the entire area with no fear of the blood running all the way to the street and leading to one of her nosy neighbors becoming curious. She stands at attention with the hose, waiting for the crimson water to turn pink and finally clear as it snakes around the top of the drain.

She sprays down everything, including the inside of her SUV. Being diligent in the cleaning aspect is the sole reason Shannon believes she has been getting away with this as long as she has. Not only does it keep her out of jail, but the extra time allows for the snakes to finish up their meals and return to their normal existence. The fingers are all gathered up and placed inside a bag, which Shannon places securely in her chest pocket. She remembers the first time the smaller snakes, especially Lucky, allowed her to hand feed them. It was the closest thing she has ever felt to the feeling a mother has while breast feeding their children. If she were to talk to anyone about her reptile kids, which she would never do, she would try to convince them that she could see the love and affection in the eyes of Lucky and the small ball python when she fed them. Yes, sometimes she thinks she's crazy for living her life this way.

Other times, when she has looked the children in the eyes, she wouldn't change her life for the world.

Satisfied that the area has been cleaned up to her liking, Shannon heads into the loneliness of her home. It's the empty bedrooms, the silence as she enters, that makes her keep the snakes around. She considers them her family, and like any mother, she wants to make sure that her kids have eaten all their meal. She opens the basement door and looks down the stairs. Her look is returned by the milky eyes of Powder, the giant albino Burmese python. She can tell just by looking at the creature that he is moving with more energy, an obvious sign that he enjoyed his meal. Feeling triumphant, Shannon takes the stairs two at a time and finds her familiar seat in the easy chair tucked in the corner of the damp space. She looks around at her reptile children and smiles with content. There is not a single trace of the two women she tossed down here a few minutes earlier.

7 Days in Hell

4

Lucky is the first to slither his way over to her. He assumes his customary position on her right shoulder, curling up and looking up at her. Monty, the small ball python, works his way up her leg and nestles himself in the crevice of her lap. She finds it odd that she can see no trace of the body parts as she looks around the room. Usually, she could see small morsels of muscle or tissue that had not yet been claimed by the snakes when she sits down. Maybe these women were too skinny. Shannon begins to worry if her children got enough to eat or maybe some of them are still a little hungry. The smell of human flesh is still heavy in the stagnant air, but the reptiles have cleaned every morsel of skin and muscle from the floor.

As she looks the smaller snakes in the eyes and tells them about the confrontation with the police officer, she pulls the bag of bloody fingers from her pocket. The rustling of the plastic draws the attention of the remaining snakes, and as she feeds the digits to the two smaller reptiles, she begins to draw a crowd. The normally shy iguana has even snuck out from his hiding place and taken up a position near Shannon's chair, hoping to snatch up any morsels that may hit the ground. She only gives the bigger snakes a passing glance, knowing they have all eaten already and she enjoys the one on one time she is sharing with her favorite snakes.

Shannon loves allowing Lucky to eat the bloody fingers directly from the palm of her hand. Watching his mouth open and digest the finger whole is something she never gets tired of seeing. She can hear the tiny bones in the finger crunch under the pressure of the internal organs of the snake, the sound reminding Shannon of fingers snapping. As she nears the end of the bag of finger nuggets, Powder has worked his way along a sewage pipe and has begun to hang a few feet over her head. She is oblivious to his presence and simply continues to hold fingers in the palm of her hand. As she waits for Lucky to grab the final finger, her attention is drawn to movement above her. When she first looks up and realizes that Powder has been hovering there, she begins to panic. He has never come this close to her while she was feeding the smaller ones. When the enormous weight of his body drops directly on top of her, she screams in fright.

The two-hundred-pound reptile knocks Shannon from her seat and onto the floor, her body crashing with an audible thug against the cold ground. She tries to scramble quickly, reaching for anything to help her get back to her feet. As if fired from slingshots, the larger snakes in the room move quickly toward her. Powder has wrapped himself around her legs, his massive muscles tightening and forcing her feet together. She tries desperately to loosen his grip, but he is just too massive to manhandle. Another large python has started to wrap his body around her neck. She successfully uncoils him once but is unable to completely remove him from on top of her. She feels the sharp stinging pain of the iguana taking a large chunk out of the hand she has been using to balance her body on the floor. She manages to yank her hand away and sees the blood dripping from her fingers. She knows the effect the scent of blood will have on these creatures. Much like sharks, these snakes work themselves into a frenzy whenever they smell blood, refusing to stop until they have captured and swallowed their prey.

She tries to scream, but much like her ability to breathe, the words have left her body. The snakes begin to tighten their grip and Shannon once again hears the familiar sound of fingers snapping. Powder has worked his way up her torso and has started squeezing her abdomen, cracking every one of her ribs in the process. The near silent hissing coming from the animals adds fear to an already horrific situation. She can only raise her hands slightly at this point. The sight of the chunk of flesh missing from her palm makes her begin to cry. When she looks at her bloody hand again, her fingers look very similar to those she was feeding to Lucky just a few minutes earlier. As if on cue, the bright green snake clamps down on her middle finger and begins gnawing on her finger while shaking his body frantically.

She can no longer defend herself against these reptiles. The one that she had fought off from around her neck, now has worked his way around her head. She had never envisioned the strength of the snakes would be as strong as this. She knew these creatures were dangerous, but they were her family. Never in a million years would she think they would turn against her. Shannon is beginning to lose vision as her eyes are literally beginning to bulge from the sockets. Her chest is straining with each attempt to inhale precious air, losing the tug of war with the massive white snake. Her mouth is beginning to fill with a mixture of blood and vial, the rancid combination being forced into her mouth as her internal organs begin to burst. Powder curls around a final time and positions his face near her chest. She looks at him through the last light that remains in her vision. The snake looks to be smiling at her as he tenses his body a final time. The sound of her back and neck snapping echo through the basement almost simultaneously. Like the ones before her, there is nothing left of Shannon once the reptiles have finished their feeding frenzy. Every morsel is digested in the matter of a few minutes. The basement returns to the calm reptile sanctuary it had been since the first snake was brought into the home.

7 Days in Hell

OFF THE TRAIL

JEFF'S STORY

1

When it comes to breathtaking views and mesmerizing scenery, there isn't a better place in the country than the Appalachian Trail. The over two-thousand-mile trail stretches from Georgia to Maine and crosses through fourteen states. The rise and fall in altitude make some of the trail almost impossible for average hikers, while thousands of more experienced hikers relish the challenge of the troublesome terrain. One of the most common misconceptions of the trail is that most of it is found in the middle of nowhere. The truth is, that on average, the trail crosses a road about every four miles. There are still hundreds of thousands of uninhabited acres that surround the trail, but for the most part, visitors stay within the trail that is clearly marked with little white stakes. Jeff, on the other hand, is not like most visitors.

He has always danced to the beat of his own drum. If you have ever seen him dance, you would know that the drum he is dancing to is a little out of tune. Even when the entire dance floor is doing the electric slide, you can find Jeff in the middle of the floor, bouncing up and down with his arms out to his side. He has lived against the grain since childhood, and since turning eighteen, Jeff has taken a weeklong trip to the Appalachian Trail. He doesn't consider himself an avid outdoorsman, but he loves the solitude that goes along with the trek. His wife understood this about her husband when they got married, and although she has protested every year, Jeff has continued to make the solo journey.

This year, he has decided to visit the portion of the trail that snakes through West Virginia. Everyone has heard the stories of some of the strange people who live in the hills in the area, but this is his fifteenth-year hiking alone and he has yet to encounter any locals that he would consider a threat. The closest he ever came to danger was when he stumbled upon an old moonshining still in the foothills of Kentucky. After finding the still, he quickly retraced his steps until he was back on the marked trail. He never told his wife this story, knowing that she would freak out and give him even more grief when it was time for his annual trip the next year.

As much as he likes walking along the trail, Jeff loves breaking away from the marked path even more. He loves the feeling of getting almost lost and being surrounded by nothing but nature. There's a serenity to knowing that even if you screamed at the top of your lungs, the only thing that would happen is you would scare away a few birds. He packed extremely light for his walk today, nothing more than a few snacks and water in his backpack. He set up camp at the bottom of the steep hill yesterday and set off toward the peak early in the morning. A fellow hiker, a young woman named Robyn, had told him about a small waterfall she found about a mile from the summit, and Jeff had every intention on finding it. When he veered from the path halfway to the summit, he was instantly met with thick vines covered in tiny little thorns. The cargo pants his wife insisted he pack were now coming in handy, something else he would surely not bring up to her when he got home.

After pushing through the dense foliage for a few hundred feet, the walking becomes easier. The tall trees, thick branches and massive canopy provide shade from the rising sun and the scorching temperatures that follow. Jeff takes long breaks a few times every hour. He likes to have time to take in his surroundings. It's one thing to say you have hiked the Appalachian Trail. It's another thing entirely to spend enough time to garner appreciation for your surroundings. He listens to the birds. The rustling of falling leaves let him know that the wildlife is just as active in the area as he is.

He is climbing the same ridge as the marked trail but moving on a slightly different line. Instead of going straight over the top of the hill, when he left the path, he headed up the mountain sideways. It allowed him to reach the same mountaintop, just a few hundred feet further to the west. It also had the added benefit of not tiring him out as quickly, since he was climbing at a less strenuous incline. In all the years of taking these trips, he has never worried about getting lost. He knows there are small mountain towns every few miles. That knowledge, and the fact that he has lived in a big city all his life, where people have no idea how isolated some parts of the country can be, has given Jeff a false sense of security and direction. If something were to happen, all he would need to do is make his way back down the hill and he would eventually come across the marked path.

After two hours of strenuous uphill hiking, he comes across a small opening in the trees. The area looks as if the trees had been intentionally cleared away, although there are no stumps or any other sign that trees once stood here. He doesn't see the waterfall the woman had told him about but there is a small pond, no larger than a softball field. He saunters over to the edge of the water and can see several large bass swimming through the shallow waters. The sight of the fish causes an instant pang in his stomach. The thought of eating fresh caught fish instead of the canned tuna in his backpack is overpowering. He pulls the retractable rod and reel from his bag and after kicking over a few rocks, he finds a small worm to thread onto his hook. With a simple flick of his wrist he casts his line into the water.

No sooner had the line hit the water and he had his first fish hooked. Jeff was giddy with excitement. He had brought the small rod and reel on every trip he has taken and never had the chance to use it. The first fish he brought in was barely larger than the palm of his hand. He released it and cast his line out again. In the course of ten minutes, Jeff had managed to land several decent size fish. He released them all, knowing that he would not be able to eat more than one. If he decided to keep the first one he caught, there would be no point in continuing to fish, and he was having too much fun. He was so caught up in the fishing, that he failed to notice the dark clouds that had drifted overhead. They began to encompass the small opening of the forest in shadow, making it increasingly difficult for him to see his line in the water. The inability to keep an eye on his line was the only thing that drew his attention to the sky.

He continues to monitor the weather while repeatedly bringing fish onto the bank in rapid succession. At the very last instance, just when he thought the skies were about to open, Jeff landed the biggest fish of the afternoon. It was so large that he thought he was going to snap his line. He managed to get the monster onto the shore, and with a quick glance at the sky, decided this was going to be his meal. He collapsed the reel and tucked it away in the leg pocket on his pants. With the large fish in one hand and rumbling thunder roaring closer by the second, he quickly looked for the best place to take cover from the impending downpour. He had planned to start a fire and cook his lunch but with the rain coming, he would have to find somewhere with enough cover from the downpour to allow for a fire.

How he had not seen it earlier was a surprise to Jeff. Tucked under the branches of a tall oak, practically built right into the trunk, was a small wooden structure, the walls nothing more than wilted pieces of old lumber. In his mind, Jeff didn't even consider that someone would actually live in the rundown shack. There is hardly a roof left, and the part of the roof that does remain, provides very little protection from the elements. Jeff didn't need somewhere to live though. He simply needed somewhere to get out of the storm and cook his lunch. Somewhere dry enough to allow him to start a fire and wait out the rain.

He walks quickly around the pond, as the first drops of rain fall onto his lucky visor. The hat has seen its fair share of rainstorms. It's an old visor with a beer logo on the front, the former navy blue now faded to several different shades other than navy. The sweat ring around the edges has turned the cloth a bleach stained off-white, but the hat has gotten him through two marriages, and he's worn it on every hike. His pace quickens even more when he hears the crackle of lightning nearby. He pauses briefly about ten feet from the shack, taking in its deplorable conditions. What once was a door is now nothing more than a piece of wood that is leaning haphazardly against a dark opening. The lone window next to the door is cracked and grime covered, making it impossible to see anything on the inside. The pouring rain has forced him to move more quickly than he normally would have, meaning he failed to notice the bloodshot eye that was peeking out through the broken window. He had no idea that the person on the inside of the run-down shack had been watching his every move since he entered the clearing and started fishing. Just before he enters the shack, the eye blinks and disappears into the darkness of the room behind the glass.

7 Days in Hell

2

The rain is coming down in buckets. It's the kind of rain that forms puddles on the ground instantly, no matter how dry the dirt was before the storm. Jeff uses his boot to kick open the sheet of wood covering the opening to the shack. It falls to the side of the building in a thump that is barely heard over the sound of the rain pelting the walls and what's left of the roof of the structure. As he steps inside, the overall darkness and the foul odor are the first things he notices. Even with the large opening in the wall, there is hardly any natural light to help with visibility. As the storm intensifies, the winds also begin to pick up. Jeff notices the large holes in the roof that are responsible for the gallons of water seeping through.

The side of the room nearest the door opening is mostly covered and Jeff focuses his attention on this side. As he looks around the area, he is trying to hold his breath, refusing to allow the putrid smell of death to enter his nasal passages. As his eyes begin to adjust to the darkness, he finds nothing out of the ordinary. In fact, most of what he can see looks to be in the same condition as the shack itself. The small, round table looks like it might have been made by hand, but it's so old and unmaintained that it is barely standing. Dust covers the surface, making it impossible for Jeff to use it to prep the fish he intended to cook.

He faces the opposite side of the room and through the openings in the roof and what little light is coming through the broken window, he can see the rain is beginning to let up. It only rained hard for a few minutes, but the entire floor of the rundown shack is covered in water, making the dirt floor a muddy mess. He looks around for a rag or some piece of cloth that he can use to clean off the surface of the small table. He can hear the mud squish below his boot as he walks the four paces to the other side. He bangs his shin into the foot of a makeshift bed, not being able to see it tucked in the corner of the room. As he bends to rub his leg, his eyes are drawn to the small stuffed bear on the bed. On one leg of the animal, dark tape has been used to cover a rip in the stitching. The thing looks terrifying in the darkness, its eyes matching the intensity of the weather outside. What is supposed to bring comfort to small children has had the opposite effect on Jeff.

He has a hard time taking his eyes away from the bear, but he grabs for the tattered blanket and sweeps it away from the mattress. He wraps the blanket around the fish and lays them both on the dusty table. His next matter of business is finding something inside the structure that would be suitable to start a fire. Once again, his stare returns to the bed. The frame looks to be untreated wood, probably sourced from the woods right outside the front door. Jeff kicks at the thin wooden poles at the foot of the bed and sees the whole structure rattle with minimal effort. His plan is to break the bed apart into manageable pieces and position the wood directly under one of the openings in the roof. This will allow the resulting smoke to exit through the roof, preventing the room from filling with the toxic fumes.

As he walks around to the head of the bed, the clanging sound of his foot kicking something metallic on the floor startles him. The old coffee can tips over and brown sludgy liquid pours from it. Even though the thought of having his boots covered in whatever bodily fluid was in that can makes him nauseous, Jeff is relieved to finally find out what had been responsible for the foul stench that had nearly gagged him when he first stepped inside. He nonchalantly kicks the can to the far corner of the room, as far away from where he intends to start his fire as he can get it. Next, he reaches down with both hands and grabs the thin mattress. As he tosses the flimsy thing into the same corner as the soiled coffee can, he can see the there are only a few wood slats that kept the bed intact. As he turns his head to look closer at the bed frame, he notices the large lump covered by a blanket between the slats that held the mattress and the dirt floor. A small portion of his brain, somewhere way in the back that still remembers his near miss with the moonshiners in the past, thinks there could be someone living in this building. The larger portion of his mind tells him there is no way a person could survive in these conditions.

Jeff hesitantly reaches his hands through the slats and grabs ahold of the blanket, his fist grasping the cloth tightly. In a single motion, he raises his hand above his head. The dust that escapes forms a cloud over the area making it difficult to see what had formed the mass on the ground. A cough escapes his mouth as the mustiness of the air enters his sinuses. After quickly fanning his hand from side to side, Jeff looks down on what was below the bed, and what he sees causes every hair on his arms to stand at attention.

Initially, they stare at each other. The frail looking girl huddled under the bed, obviously fearful of the stranger who had come here and started tearing things up. The longer they stare at each other, neither attempting to make a sound, the quicker Jeff's heart begins to race. He doesn't know what to say to this girl. It's hard to see much of her, but he's guessing she is no more than ten or eleven years old. Her skin is very pale, and he can make out several of her ribs through her torn night gown. Her long black hair is matted and stuck to the sides of her face, the dampness from the rain forcing the strands against her head. After what seemed like an eternity, Jeff finally breaks the stare.

He doesn't say anything. Instead, he decides to remove the frame of the bed from over top of the girl in hopes that she will see that he is not there to do her harm. The frame is light, and he is easily able to pick it up and move it to the opposite side of the room. He only struggles slightly to get the frail structure to stand against the opposite wall. He expected to see the girl still huddled in a ball on the ground when he turned around. He expected her to remain quiet. When he turned around and she was standing, with her ghost-like face looking right at him, he nearly screamed. When she stretched out her arm and began to walk toward him, Jeff ran as quickly as he could from the dilapidated shack, refusing to look back.

3

"Paw Paw gonna kill you! Paw Paw gonna kill you!"

The screams from the girl whistle through the trees and chase him no matter how quickly he moves. Jeff always claimed to be fast, but he is much older now and the few years of smoking he did when he was younger have left him breathless after only a few strides. He pushes on, hoping to get as far away from the creepy little girl as he can. The rain has made every step a treacherous one. Only seconds after getting out of the cabin, Jeff was able to make it into the trees and brush. It will be much harder for the little girl to chase him through the thick growth, but it also slows down his own progress. His body is moving faster than it has moved in years and he is paying no attention to which direction he is going. He knows that he is going down the side of hill, but he can't remember if he is near the path that led him to the clearing or if he is on the entire other side. If he is on the wrong side, it could mean that when he gets to the bottom, he could be as far as five miles away from where his campsite is. While being so far away from his tent isn't ideal, getting away from the screaming girl is the only thought going through his mind.

He stops momentarily, trying to gauge his surroundings and make heads or tails out of where he is on the mountain. He learned long ago how to navigate by using the direction of the sun, but the weather is not cooperating. Even on a sunny day it would be hard to peer through the dense coverage of the pine and oak trees. Satisfied that he is descending on the proper side he tries to catch his breath, giving him time to think more clearly about what just happened. There was no sign that someone had been living in the shack. He had no way of knowing that the little girl was going to be in there. Even when he walked into the shack, she was hiding, so he was just as startled as she was when he pulled her blanket away. The ability to slow down the events have helped make his fear subside, and the problem-solving portion of his brain begins to make a mental inventory of what he has available. This is when he notices that he is no longer carrying his backpack. He must have left it laying on the table next to the fish he had wrapped in the blanket. He reaches up and feels for his lucky visor, thankful when he touches the familiar cloth.

He begins to frantically go through his pockets. He has his utility knife, which has its own fire starter, which could come in handy. He finds the collapsible fishing pole in his pants pocket, along with his small flashlight, the latter being the only thing that might help him navigate his way off this mountain if he gets stuck up here once the sun goes down. He puts the items back into his pockets, making certain to keep the flashlight in a pocket that he could get to in a hurry if needed. A quick scan of the terrain around him and Jeff decides on the direction he needs to head to make the easiest descent. The forest on this side of the hill is much thicker than what he made his way through to get up the mountain, so he moves slowly, making sure his footing in the damp mud is firm before proceeding.

As he walks, his mind continues to bring up the images of the little girl. When he first spotted her, she looked so frail and helpless. Her night gown was loose and ill-fitting, but there was no mistaking the ridges left in the fabric from her ribs. When she made it to her feet, and began walking toward him, she looked completely different. Her face showed a little more color and her eyes seemed to glow red. It seemed she had been possessed or gathered strength from somewhere in the few seconds he had his back turned toward her. He hadn't really thought about the words she screamed as he was running away; he was too busy trying to get as far away as he could. Now that he has time to think about what she said, the thought that she might have a father living in that shack only solidifies the fact that he needs to get out of the area quickly. The little girl he could probably handle, but whoever this Paw Paw character she referred to is, would probably be a bigger issue. He could hardly believe that a small child would be living in the shack, meaning it's even harder to believe that two people would be living there. He clearly heard the girl's words and there is no doubt in his mind she was calling for someone else.

After twenty minutes of labored walking through fallen branches, deep puddles and slippery footing, Jeff finally makes his way out onto a foot path. It's not a very wide path, and definitely not the same one he was on going up the hill, but he is undoubtedly getting closer to making his way out of the woods and away from the girl and her shack. Jeff picks his pace up slightly with the surer footing. He has been through too much and lost too much energy to continue creating his own path through the woods, so he stays on the footpath. He will have to make his way to his campsite from wherever this path leads him. His body is starting to growl as the late afternoon sun finally makes a brief but welcoming appearance. He looks up to the sky to judge his direction, hoping to guesstimate where this path is leading him. When the sun disappears behind another large cloud, he returns his attention to the solitude of the West Virginia dirt in front of him.

The sides of the path have become increasingly narrow as he has walked along, the weeds and vines inching out from the forest toward the walkway. Like anyone who hasn't eaten in almost a full day, Jeff allows his mind to drift to thoughts of smokes bass and how good it would have been to have cooked the fish he had caught. The daydreaming had taken full command of his head as his body moved along without much authority. As the path turned sharply to the right, Jeff was barely paying attention. His lack of focus causes his heart to skip a beat when he hears the now familiar voice of the little girl. She is standing all alone, directly in front of him. The tattered and torn stuffed bear is resting peacefully in her right arm as she rubs her dirty fingers across its head. The words tear through Jeff's mind like nails on a chalkboard.

"There he is Paw Paw. There he is!"

7 Days in Hell

4

Jeff stands frozen in the middle of the narrow walkway. His eyes dart from side to side, trying to get a glimpse of the infamous Paw Paw this girl keeps screaming about. He has still yet to see anyone else, but the sight of the girl is the only thing Jeff needed to motivate him to get moving. He was further nudged forward when the little girl took off in a sprint toward him, her bare feet slamming loud on the dirt ground as her torn night gown flows loosely around her skinny frame. Like a cat that has been startled awake, Jeff throws his body into the air and over the edge on the side of the path. His legs move quickly, barely contacting the ground as he barrels through the thick brush.

The footing is muddy and damp, causing him to fly down the side of the hill at a faster speed than he would normally feel safe to descend. His heart is racing, beating as if ready to explode from his chest, and he can still hear the words from the little girl behind him. She is howling like an Indian on the warpath. Her words rain down from above as Jeff tries frantically to get down the hill. Gravity has gotten the best of him and he is no longer in control of his body.

His only hope is to keep his balance and remain upright. Just when he thinks he has lost the battle and will go tumbling down the hill out of control, he is able to grab ahold of a large branch. The desperate move slows his momentum, but at the expense of shredding the soft skin on his palms and possibly pulling his left shoulder out of socket. He can feel the muscles in his shoulder tear as he lowers his arms to his side once his body has stopped moving.

The pain is searing in his arm, but Jeff manages to get himself moving down the hill once again. He tries to be more patient now that his adrenaline has returned to a normal level and he can no longer hear the loud squeals from the creepy girl. He still has never seen the person she has been calling for, but he doesn't want to wait around for the man to show up. No matter how slowly he tries to move, the precarious footing and steepness of the hill make it difficult to control his pace. This time when his body begins to move faster than his legs, he tumbles head over heels. Jeff does several painful somersaults and cartwheels, bouncing off the trunks of large trees with his body crashing through large patches of thorn bushes along the way. When he comes to an abrupt halt in an unnatural position, he is relieved to finally be stopped. When the pain makes its way from his leg to his brain, Jeff screams in agony and nearly loses consciousness.

He has landed in the mud on his stomach with his face looking down the side of the mountain, his lucky visor twisted sideways on his head. Every movement of his body causes a stabbing pain to shoot up his right leg, a pain that causes his entire body to shiver. He has no problem moving his left leg, but his injured right leg is pinned somehow. The mud under his body makes it difficult to gain any traction with his scraped-up palms as he tries to push his body backwards. He is trying to position himself so he can at least assess the injury and free himself from whatever has his leg trapped. After a long struggle, he manages to maneuver his body in a manner that will allow him to see his right leg. The sight of it is nauseating.

During his tumble down the hill, somehow his right foot became wedged in the root of a large pine tree. The root protrudes from the ground and breaks off in two separate directions in a V pattern. Jeff's foot was wedged in the V in a precarious position. On top of being trapped, the force and momentum of the accident snapped the femur in his leg. The jagged and bloody edge of the bone has pierced through the muscle and poked a hole clear through his cargo pants. To add insult to injury, Jeff's ankle is twisted so badly that his foot is pointing up the hill when the rest of his body is facing in the opposite direction, as if his foot is one backwards. Just looking at the damage to his leg almost makes him throw up once again, and if he had any food in his system, he probably would. He has no other option but to try and get his foot free from the gnarly root and somehow try to get down the hill. Thoughts of his wife and kids flash through his vision, doing their best to mask the pain.

The sweat drips from his forehead as he tries to reach out for his right foot. Jeff takes a pause long enough to remove his visor and wipe the sweat away with his forearm. He keeps his eyes on the boot, forcing himself to avoid looking at the bone protruding from his leg. The pain is like nothing he has ever felt before. For a moment he thinks about removing his boot but thinks better of it when he realizes that would only make things worse for the pain in his ankle. With no other way left to free his foot, he grits his teeth and makes a final lunge for his boot. With a sharp snap, the foot comes free and his body is once again sliding down the side of the hill. This trip is far more painful but luckily doesn't last as long. After only a few seconds, the back of his head bangs against a tree trunk and his body stops. He has just enough time to look up at the beams of sunlight that are sneaking through the trees before his body gives up and he passes out.

5

"Paw Paw! Here he is!"

Jeff struggles to open his eyes, hopeful that the girl's voice is something left over from a dream. When he raises his head, his sees the girl standing ten feet in front of him. Her bloodshot eyes look more demonic now than they have all day. They now seem to glow as darkness has begun to settle over this side of the hill. Jeff finds it hard to see her and rubs his eyes to remove the remaining blurriness. If he had hoped clearing his vision would make her disappear, he was dead wrong. The girl remains standing in the same spot she was a few seconds earlier, only now, she is swaying with excitement and spinning around with her stuffed bear. Although she was dingy and dirty when he first found her in the shack, now she looks like she has slid into every mud puddle she found. Her bare feet are caked with flaky brown dirt and her once light-colored night gown is now soiled completely though.

He has no energy to try to get away, even trying to move slightly only sends lightning bolts of pain through his aching body. He looks down at his leg and notices the bugs have begun to feast on his flesh. Flies, ants and even a few maggots have invaded the area where the bone tore through his flesh and pants. Jeff, defeated and exhausted, doesn't even try to shoo them away. He returns his gaze to the girl, who seems to be giddy with excitement. Jeff looks at her with a father's eyes, a father who has a daughter who is not much younger than the child in front of him. A father who couldn't imagine the circumstances that would force a person to raise a child like this. The intensity of the day's events had made it hard for him to realize he was running from a girl who is a third of his size and no matter what kind of life she has been living and no matter how much she has had to struggle, she is still a child. He also thinks about his own little girl and the active imagination that kids have. This girl in the woods has been yelling all day for someone named Paw Paw and Jeff is starting to think that maybe this person doesn't exist. It wouldn't be too far-fetched for this little girl to have an imaginary friend to keep her company. Who knows how long she could have been living in that shack alone? Who knows what living in conditions like that for a long period would do to a young child's mind?

"We're gonna eat you. Paw Paw gonna cut you up good." Her voice is child-like, but the words are ominous and cut through the night air. The twang

and drawl of her voice is so deep that every word she speaks sounds like it has a few extra syllables.

The two remain focused on each other for several seconds, neither wanting to take their eyes off the other. Jeff is the first to faulter, choosing to look behind him for a possible escape route. There was no sense sitting here and looking at the girl any longer. She had yet to do him any harm, all his injuries to this point were caused by him running away. He was also not a hundred percent convinced that there was anyone named Paw Paw. If there wasn't, he still needed to find a way down this mountain. He begins to push his body, using only his hands and one good leg. It would take a long time to get to the bottom like this, but he saw no other option and no sense in prolonging the journey. As he slides away, he looks back at the girl one last time. Her focus is still on him, but her swaying has stopped. She turns her head slightly and for the first time looks away from Jeff's face. The bloodshot eyes of the girl look past him and seem to grow bigger by the second.

Before he could turn his head to see what had drawn her attention, he feels the rough skin of a hand on his throat. The pressure instantly takes his breath away. There is no mistaking the power of whoever has ahold of his neck and the hand is well worked, as if the person has hands of leather. Without much effort, the hand around his neck raises his entire body off the ground. His injured leg sways grotesquely from side to side. He hears a male grunt from behind, but the vice-like grip on his neck makes it impossible to turn around. It would take an idiot to think that the person was anyone other than the infamous Paw Paw person this little girl has been calling all day.

The girl begins to sway again as she starts humming a tune, her soft tones only being heard between gasps of air as Jeff struggles to breath. He is forced to look at her and is completely at the mercy of the man behind him. She begins to nod her head frantically, grabbing long strands of her black hair and using it to shield her eyes as she does so. This is the first time all day when she actually resembled the small child that she was. Jeff, realizing what is about to happen, begins to kick with his only working leg. He shakes violently trying to free himself from the man's powerful grasp, but only manages to cause himself more pain. The man simply puts his second hand around Jeff's neck to combat the gyrations and effectively eliminating any chance of Jeff wiggling free.

At this point, the only thing Jeff is hoping for is that the end comes swift and quick. His pain tolerance has always been low, and right now he is experiencing excruciating pain. His vision begins to diminish, a dark black ring surrounding everything his eyes see, including the little girl who is practically dancing in front of him. His wish of a swift death comes shortly after, as the man swings his arm and slams Jeff's head into the side of the tree. The thud of his skull striking the side of the tree echoes through the woods and causes the evil little girl to squeal in delight. The first blow worked perfectly in knocking Jeff out. It took several more whacks against the tree before his skull cracked and its milky contents began to ooze out. The large man throws the lifeless body over his shoulder and the two begin the long uphill climb back to their cabin, the little girl sporting a new lucky beer visor on her head. She didn't care that the hat was covered in blood and she only stopped long enough to grab the stuffed bear. She tosses the toy over her shoulder and starts walking up the hill, just like her Paw Paw.

7 Days in Hell

DINNER AND DEATH

JESSICA'S STORY

7 Days in Hell

1

A blind date can be an excruciating experience. The thought of getting dressed up to share a fancy meal with a complete stranger is not something most people look forward to, that is, unless you're Jessica. She has been so caught up in her professional life that she has failed to keep up with her friends when it comes to creating a family. She has started to believe that she will only be able to meet men that her married girlfriends set her up with. A large portion of these dates have been brutal, with the rare exception. The last one, a guy she met at a New Year's Eve party, seemed to be really into her. Before the end of the night they were getting physical in the laundry room of the house. Unfortunately, the relationship fizzled when they both realized that they had little in common other than the physical attraction, and Jessica refocused her attention to her job.

Her friend Robyn had assured her that this guy would be perfect for her, and even if he wasn't, Jessica was happy to have something to get her out of the house. His name was Anthony and he was some sort of corporate attorney, Robyn didn't know too many more details. He was described as being just as involved in his career as Jessica was, apparently attractive in his own way and funny. She can't help but to smile as she drives away from the restaurant, satisfied that the evening could not have gone any better. They talked, laughed, and even sang along to the Mariachi band that played at their table. Anthony would surely be a hit with Jessica's mother, who has always been a sucker for a man who speaks Spanish.

They had talked long after most of the diners had left for the evening and it wasn't until the waitress let them know the restaurant was closing that they had realized how long they had been there. He walked Jessica to her car and was even gentleman enough to allow her to use his jacket as protection from the rain. The rain had stopped as they reached her car but there was no way she was going to let mother nature dictate how the end of this perfect date was going to go. Before closing her car door, she reached up and grabbed Anthony by the tie and pulled him into her. Their lips met and the electricity she had hoped to feel sent shockwaves through her body. She turns up the radio as she exits the highway and makes the turn toward her house, singing along to the upbeat country song that pours from the speakers as she thinks about that kiss.

It had been a few months since her fling with the laundry room guy, but the chemistry she felt in the moments after this kiss were different. It wasn't pure lust that had her wanting more. It was a connection she felt, as if she had known this man her whole life. Even thinking about the kiss now makes the butterflies return to her stomach. If it wasn't so late, she would call Robyn and thank her for putting the two of them together. She makes a mental note to thank her friend first thing in the morning.

As she pulls into the driveway of her small ranch house, she gets out of the car and is greeted with a cool spring breeze. The rain has forced away the humid air and replaced it with cooler temperatures and gentle winds. She leaves the front door open but latches the screen door behind her as she enters, hoping to fill the house with the clean night air. She had one too many margaritas at the restaurant, so she heads to the kitchen for a glass of water and some aspirin. If her college years taught her anything, it's the importance of fighting a hangover before it has time to attack. As she throws the pills in her mouth and gulps the water, she hears the ring of her cell phone in her handbag.

She doesn't recognize the number and answers the phone with a slight tone of trepidation. "Hello, this is Jessica."

The unfamiliar male voice on the other line coughs once before speaking. "Hi Jessica, this is Anthony."

The butterflies instantly return to her stomach and her smile brightens at the thought of the man. His voice doesn't sound like it did at dinner, but she thinks that could easily be caused by a poor cellular connection.

"I hope you don't mind but I got your number from Robyn. I've been trying to reach you all night," the man says.

Jessica puts down her glass of water, her smile turning down to a quizzical look. "I don't mind that she gave you my number. I had a great time tonight."

There is a long pause on the line, a more prolonged silence than they had the entire length of dinner. Anthony finally breaks the silence in his deep but calm voice, "that's why I've been trying to reach you. My flight got cancelled and I was stuck on the runway in Chicago all night. I'm just now leaving the airport. I'm really sorry"

"Is this some kind of joke?" Jessica is stunned by what the man said but the reality of it has yet to sink in.

"I wish it was. I'm sure Robyn told you how busy my life can be. I was supposed to be home this afternoon, in plenty of time to meet you. Unfortunately, the airline had different plans."

"But we ate dinner together. We laughed together. I even kissed you," Jessica said, her mind slowly putting together the pieces. "If it wasn't you, then who in the hell did I just have dinner with?"

"I can't answer that," Anthony replies.

She had been pacing the hallway between the front door and the kitchen as the phone call had been going on. She hadn't noticed the car that was parked in front of her house until the man in the driver's seat got out and started walking toward her front door.

"Anthony, I have to let you go. There is someone walking toward my house." She had begun to move her finger to the button that would hang up the phone when she heard the panicked voice of the man on the other end.

"Wait" he shouted, his voice loud enough to be heard without the phone to her ear. It makes her stop and listen closer. "Jessica do you know the man?"

"I don't know. It's dark and I can't see him yet."

"I don't like the sound of this. Is your door locked" he asks?

"Yes. Well the screen door is," she says in a timid voice.

"Close the door and lock it. Your next call should be to the police."

Jessica stands in the entryway to her home, watching the man walk toward her in the darkness. Her phone is still in her hand as she sees the familiar stroll of the dark shadow, the same walk that sauntered up to her at the restaurant bar a few hours ago. Small pieces begin to fit into the puzzle in the next few seconds. How the man never introduced himself at dinner. How she had assumed when he sat down next to her that he was Anthony and how he looked nothing like how her friend had described him. She stands silent, with only a flimsy screen door keeping him outside her house. This man who betrayed her trust and presented himself as someone who he wasn't and has now followed her to her home.

Her breaths are rapid and heavy as she brings her phone to her ear once more, "it's him. It's the man I had dinner with."

2

Jessica had been motionless as she watched the man climb the four steps to her porch. She considers herself to be a pretty good judge of character for the most part. How could her instincts have let her down so horribly tonight? She stares at the man, not sure what to do next, as he walks across the front porch to her door. She hears the mumbled static coming from her cell phone and it snaps her back to reality. She lunges for the heavy wooden door and starts to slam it shut. She was a split second too late as the man on the porch sends his fist flying through the screen door, stopping the momentum of the heavier door before Jessica could close and lock it.

The force of the man's arm stopping the swinging of the large door, sent Jessica flailing backwards, her phone falling from her hand as she hit the hardwood floor. As she turns her head, she sees the man she shared dinner and a passionate kiss with, enter her home unwarranted. He moves quickly as he closes the door behind himself and steps over her, slamming his boot on top of her phone several times. The device crumbles and small pieces of hard plastic go flying through the hallway. Confident that the phone is no longer operational and a threat to him, the man makes his way to her, slowly and confidently.

Her hands are trembling as she tries to use them to wipe the tears from her face. Her mind is still combating the polar opposites she has felt for this man in the last hour. From feeling as if she wanted to start a serious relationship with him on the ride home from dinner, to fearing for her life as he nears her. She tries to calm herself, convinced if she does this her demeanor will somehow transfer to the man and calm him as well. She forces long deep breaths in through her mouth while exhaling through her nose. She only has time enough to do this two or three times before the man reaches down and wraps his hand around her long auburn hair, wrenching her head to the side of his body.

As her body is spun around on the hardwood, her hair pulled tight by the man, she manages to swing around a connect with a powerful kick to his crotch. He lets out a low grumble of a moan and instantly releases his hold on her. Jessica uses this momentary freedom to stumble to her feet and begin running. Her mind was not in control of her body as her feet moved swiftly up the stairs and into her bathroom, the only room in the house that locks from the inside. She frantically searched the room for anything she could use to defend herself against this man.

There isn't much in the small bathroom that would be considered a weapon. She looks around the room with her back pressed firmly against the door. The neat and tidy space is well kept, even the trash can was emptied right before she left for the evening. She moves away from the door long enough to search the medicine cabinet and the storage under the vanity. Old jars of finger-nail polish, ancient cans of aerosol hair spray and a plastic bin full of hair bands and bows are tucked neatly inside. The sounds of footsteps can be heard over her heavy breathing, as the intruder makes his way up the stairs. Jessica frantically searches the medicine cabinet, spilling pill bottles and band-aids into the sink basin below.

She stops long enough to put her ear to the door. She can hear the man as he walks around in her bedroom, just five feet away from where she is hiding. She knows she doesn't have much time before he finds her. She steps into the tub and thinks momentarily about pulling the shower curtain and hoping he doesn't look inside. That idea lasted less than a second and she turned her attention to the tiny window. The glass blocks that make it impossible for people on the street to watch her take a shower, are also too thick for her to break through, not to mention that her body would never fit through the small opening. She was always proud of her body, complete with all the curves. Now she is cursing it for being too big to fit through a small opening that doesn't exist.

A small knock at the door startles her. The intruder has found her. He knocks several times, each one making the tiny hairs on Jessica's arms stand at attention.

"Jessica," the eerie voice from outside the door sings.

She does not reply.

"Jessica," he sings again, this time his voice getting higher with every syllable. "Let me in Jessica. I want another kiss."

If there was any doubt in her mind that this was the same person she had dinner with, and enjoyed, earlier in the night, that thought is now gone. She wants to scream at the man. She wants to tell him to get out of her house and leave her alone. Instead, she remains silent, hoping that he may think she is hiding somewhere else and leave. That doesn't happen. Every wall in the bathroom shakes as the man throws his body against the thin door. The second time he does this, she can see the door frame beginning to splinter. She moves her body so that if he gets into the room, she will be hidden briefly behind the door.

She is now facing the wall-mounted mirror and vanity that she had searched earlier. As the intruder bangs into the door a third time, something in the medicine cabinet catches her eye and an idea pops into her head. If she moved quickly enough her plan might work, but it would need to be well-timed. If it didn't work, then she was a dead woman.

7 Days in Hell

3

The intruder in her house is only seconds from breaking through the flimsy bathroom door and getting to her. Jessica is frantic when she finds the long lighter in the medicine cabinet that she uses to light the candles when she has a long soak in the tub. As she reaches down in the storage under the sink, she feels the shaking of the door again. She gives a passing glance at it and its frame and is convinced the next time he puts his body into it, the door will give way. She finds what she is looking for under the sink, an ancient relic of a hair spray aerosol can that is left over from her big hair days and positions herself next to the vanity.

If her plan is going to work, she is going to have to be face to face with the man outside the door. That is the only way that the potential fireball will have any effect on him. She struggles to ignite the long lighter, her trembling fingers finding it difficult to manipulate the child proofing mechanism. She knows that once the man breaks through the door, her time will be limited. Jessica doesn't want to have to fiddle with the lighter once he gets inside the small bathroom, so she presses the button several times and holds it down once the flame lights. In her other hand, she shakes up the aerosol can and gives the nozzle a few sprays to make sure the contents are still exiting the can properly.

She stands near the vanity, facing the nearly shattered door, with a lighter in one hand and a can of hair spray in the other. If she were to look at herself in the mirror right now, she would have no choice but to laugh at how she looks. But she is ready, or as ready as she can be. As the man throws his body into the door the final time, the remnants of the pressed wood fall to the floor in big chunks. The man looks at her with a confused expression, stunned by her combative stance and nature. Just as she planned, she sprays the aerosol can, allowing the flammable stream of liquid to fly through the flame from the lighter. The ball of fire that is created flies toward the man, causing him to stumble backwards into the hallway, screaming and grabbing at his face.

Jessica drops the lighter and hair spray and quickly climbs over the fallen door. If she can make it down the steps and out the front door, she knows her attacker will flee in fear of being caught. She doesn't look back at him as she turns the corner and begins going down the stairs.

"You bitch," the man yells!

She pays him no attention. She is focused on getting down the stairs and into the street. Its late, but her neighbors would have to come outside if they heard her yelling for help. She is only four or five steps from the landing and the front door when she hears the man above her walking. She didn't waste time turning around and checking to see how close the man is to her. Jessica is focused on the steps in front of her. She hadn't seen the man at the top of the steps, nor had she seen him throw the small wooden table down at her. It wasn't the impact from the fragile table that stunned her, it was the tumble down the last few steps and her head hitting the wall at the bottom. Through her foggy vision she can see the man walking toward her. The flames from the bathroom attack did little damage to his face, but it left his clothes singed and tattered.

When he makes his way to the landing, he greets her fallen body with a strong kick to her midsection. Jessica responds with a yelp and a gasp for air. He grabs her foot and drags her into the living room. As if she were a ragdoll, he picks her up and tosses her through the glass coffee table in front of the sofa. She can feel shards of glass piercing through the exposed skin of her legs and arms. She instinctually tries to roll away, her movement stopped when she reaches the couch. The intruder grabs her from the waist and throws her into the soft cushions, allowing her to face him and the large bay window that looks out onto the dark street.

She is drawn to the eyes of her attacker. At dinner, they had been warm and inviting. Now they look like the eyes of a man who has one thing one his mind, violence. How can a man turn so quickly from warm and considerate to deranged and crazy? She wants to talk to him. She wants to ask him if there was something that she did to make him this angry. Instead, she sits on the sofa and stares up at him. He is pacing the floor in front of her, trying to figure out what to do next. Jessica takes a small bit of relief knowing that the man hadn't expected her to be this combative. He hadn't expected her to put up a fight.

From her position on the sofa, she can see clearly out of the front window. The sight of headlights pulling in her driveway was brief, but she was thankful for that. She hoped that the man in her living room hadn't seen them. Maybe the man that called her phone, the real person she was supposed to meet at the restaurant, had somehow gotten ahold of the police. She continues to look out the window, hoping to see the rescue wagon show up in full force. Her attacker hadn't seen the headlights, but he does notice her looking out the window and he knows something is going on out there.

The intruder darts from in front of the window and presses his back against the wall next it. He peers from the side of the curtains, looking out into the darkness and getting a better view of whomever pulled into the driveway. Frustrated from whatever he sees, the man hugs the wall and positions himself on the inside of the front door. Jessica has no idea who or what the man saw through the window, she can barely keep her body upright after her fall down the stairs and being thrown through the coffee table. When she looks back at the intruder, she is surprised to see that the man is now holding a gun. She hadn't seen a gun throughout the entire ordeal, another sign that the man had intentions that were more cynical than just killing her.

Jessica eyes the door and entryway to her home with mixed feelings. She's anxious to see who is about to walk through the door, hoping the person will put an end to her nightmare. She is also fearful that the person that comes through will be walking right into an ambush. The door begins to open slowly, the gunman pressed against the wall behind it. The seconds go by in slow motion as Jessica strains her head to try and see who is coming in, and more importantly, how many men. She gets her answer quickly, and it disappoints her. The person who had pulled into her driveway entered the room and he was far less intimidating than she had hoped.

The man had only knocked slightly before opening the door, entering with a hesitant tone in his voice as he called out for Jessica. He was clad in dress slacks, an untucked shirt with a tie loosely around his neck. It didn't take long for him to see the frightened woman and her fear stopped him in his tracks. "Hi Jessica, I'm Anthony," was all he was able to get out before the intruder pistol whipped him with the butt of his gun. Anthony fell to the floor as Jessica let out a mournful gasp, her savior now as helpless as she is. Her hopes of rescue now lying motionless on the hardwood floor.

4

It didn't take long for the new man, the real Anthony, to come back to his senses. The two battered prisoners now sit side by side on the sofa. The intruder is standing in front of them, this time with the curtains drawn to block the view from the window. He has been standing in front of the pair, waving his gun around in front of him as if he was weighing his options mentally. When he had finally made up his mind, he turns to the two. Pointing the gun at Anthony he asks, "what are you doing here?"

"I came to help her," Anthony says, rubbing the back of his head. "The police are on their way."

"Ha! You expect me to believe that you were smart enough to call the cops? You walked right in here, unarmed. That doesn't sound very smart to me." The intruder gives the man on the sofa a disapproving look but never takes the barrel of the gun off him.

"I'll tell you what's not smart. Standing there in front of the window and putting the woman you've attacked in plain sight of anyone passing by. That's not smart." The new man says this in a combative manner, hoping to anger his captor and take the attention away from Jessica.

Without hesitation and with rage turning his face a dark red, the intruder squeezes the trigger. The sound echoes throughout the small living room, bouncing from one wall to another for what seemed like an eternity. The man on the sofa seemed to also move in slow motion, as the back of his head emptied its bloody contents across the back of the sofa and the wall behind it. Jessica wailed. She had never even seen a gun before, let alone watched one being used in the murder of a man sitting next to her on her own sofa. Tiny droplets of Anthony's blood had showered her face. She felt the warmth the moment it touched her skin and she scrambled to wipe every drop from her skin, the thought of the dead man's blood on her skin nauseating her. She is drawn to the sight of the slumped body on the couch. The single dark circle in the man's forehead the only sign of the trauma. His body fell backwards after impact, allowing the remainder of blood to be soaked into the dark brown cushions of the sofa.

"Jessica," the melodic voice of the killer pierces through the silence. "Do you remember what you told me at dinner?"

The scared woman puts her face in her hands and sobs, the only response to the man's question.

"Do you think your mom will still like me?"

Jessica only raises her head as she feels the man sit down on the sofa, between her and the body of Anthony. He rubs his hand on her leg, smearing some of the now drying blood from the cuts she suffered when being thrown through the table. The man uses the barrel of the gun to move some of her hair from her eyes, the warm metal making her draw back from him. He looks at her oddly, in a look that shows her the man thinks he is in complete control over the situation. The hand that was resting on her knee slowly moves up to her inner thigh. It takes every ounce of strength she has left to tighten her thigh muscles and squeeze her legs shut. She was not going to sit here on her own couch and be a helpless victim. Her mother raised her to be a fighter and that's exactly what she planned to do.

The man stiffens, forcing his hand out from in between her legs. She gives him a cold stare, which only earns her a slap in the face. A slap she would take a thousand times if it meant this man no longer had his hands on her. The relief doesn't last long. Instead of returning his hand to her leg, he uses it to rip open the top few buttons on her blouse. Jessica looks down, astonished at the speed of the man. She quickly throws her arm over her chest, her vain effort to cover the exposed cleavage. They stare at each other in a prolonged silence. She spits on the man the second she feels the warm metal of the gun slide down the exposed area of her breasts.

In response, the killer smiles and holds the gun in front of her face, signifying that he is the one with the weapon and therefore is in control. As he does this, Jessica decides now is the time to make her final stand. She propels herself from the couch and reaches for the gun with both hands, digging her nails into the man's flesh just above his wrist. As he begins to fight back, a single shot is fired into the ceiling. The wrestling match becomes more intense, Jessica matching his strength as only a woman fearing for her life can. The frantic nature of the jostling sends the two rolling off the sofa and on top of the broken remnants of the coffee table.

She was able to maintain her hold on the man's wrist as they fell to the ground. It was only after he ended up on top of her that his leverage forced her to break her grip. He looks down at her with a victorious grin, the gun still held tightly in his hand. His knees are positioned on either side of her body and his weight is making it hard for her to breath. He bends down and gives her long kiss on the mouth. She twists and curls her face trying to get away from the same lips she so passionately kissed hours earlier. When the man raises his body away from her again, they both notice the same thing and look toward the window at the same time.

Even though the curtains had been drawn and there is no way to see what is happening in the street, the flashing red and blue lights are a sure indication. Anthony was telling the truth. He had indeed called the police and they were outside. Jessica breathes a sigh of relief, knowing that the whole nightmare would be over soon. The man climbs from on top of her and again steals a peak from the corner of the curtain. Jessica uses this time to move her body away from the window, propping herself against the sofa. Whenever the killer pulls the curtain back, the amount of flashing light that enters the room lets her know that there is more than one police car in front of her house.

"Looks like you're in trouble now, big man," she says, trying to unnerve the intruder.

He lets the curtain fall back to the window and turns to her slowly. "No, Jessica. It looks like you're in trouble. I was just going to have a little fun with you. Now I have to kill you."

5

The man with the gun wastes no time. He sprints into the kitchen, leaving Jessica sitting on the floor next to sofa, helpless and not knowing what to do. She wonders what is taking the police so long to enter the house. She wonders why the intruder thought now was a good time to go to the kitchen. She hears the man in the other room slamming drawers and opening cabinets. She thinks of screaming but decides right away to remain quiet, remembering that the man is only feet away from her and he has no fear of using his gun.

It's not long before the gunman returns to the front living room, dragging one of Jessica's kitchen chairs behind him. He stops about five feet from the front door and positions the chair in the middle of the entryway. Jessica looks at him, not really sure what the man is planning to do. When he turns his body toward her, she begins to move away. Her body is beaten and battered, forcing her to groan with every labored movement. Her attacker barely even looks at her as he walks over the broken coffee table to the other side of the sofa. He uses his arm to knock the contents of the small end table onto the ground and discards the removable glass surface onto the floor. The remaining wooden frame is moved over and placed between the kitchen chair and the front door. He then moves the dead body of Anthony and positions it in the hallway near the front door, close enough that the door would not open fully without hitting the body.

The man is focused and moves with precision. Even though Jessica has no idea what the man is planning to do with the rearranged furniture, the intruder seems to have a concise plan. When he faces Jessica again, the fire in his eyes has returned. He walks straight toward her, his piercing eyes never leaving her face. As he reaches his hand out for her, she begins to pull away. The constrictions of the sofa make getting away impossible and the man latches on to her long hair. As he pulls her to her feet with one hand, his other hand is pulling a roll of duct tape from his pocket. Jessica was worried the man was reaching for his gun and is relieved to see the paisley and flower pattern of the tape, a leftover from a long-forgotten craft project.

He forces her into the chair in the entryway, quickly wrapping the duct tape around her mouth in rapid loops. In less than a second, the tape has been wrapped around her head several times, ensuring that any sound that escapes her mouth will be muffled.

Satisfied he has silenced his prisoner; the man turns his attention to her arms. He tries to pull them down so her forearms rest on either side of the wooden frame of the small end table. Whenever he puts her arms down, the fight in Jessica forces her to pull them away. After several semi-comical repetitions, the man gives up. He moves around the table and delivers two solid punches to her ribcage.

The impact of the punches forces the air from Jessica's body. Her sounds go unheard but her body doubles over, she instinctually reaches for the same wooden frame to catch herself. The attacker, having achieved his goal, moves quickly to secure her forearms to the table with the tape. He then forces her hands together by wrapping the tape around her wrists. The pain in her side is brutal and making it hard for her to breath, the tape covering her mouth adding to her respiratory issues. Before she notices what the man has done to her arms, he has already started taping her ankles to the legs of the chair.

The man finishes with her ankles and stands behind her. She is pinned to the table frame, hunched over and unable to move from the uncomfortable position. Jessica has no idea what the man is doing behind her, but she can feel his presence. The eerie silence is broken by the loud popping of gunshots. Jessica had assumed she had taken her last breath but when she opens her eyes, she is relieved to still be alive. She can see the bullet holes in the door and frame in front of her. As her ears are ringing and she continues to try and piece together what just happened, the intruder appears in front of her again. His movements are quick as he puts the chrome gun into her hands and secures it there with more tape. With her attacker standing in front of her and securing the gun in her hands, she quickly pulls the trigger several times on the gun. When nothing happens, she looks up at the man perplexed.

"Jessica," the killer says in the same melodic tone that she has grown to detest. "Give me more credit than that."

The gun is shaking in her hands. She has never held a gun before and now there is one forced into her grip. This is the final piece she needs to understand the plan her attacker has devised. As she looks down at the gun in her hands, she realizes she is forced to hold it out toward the front door, the same door the police are going to enter. The shots the man just made in the door would make that an inevitability. They would have to come in now and when they do, she will be pointing an empty gun right at them. He has set the trap and she is the bait.

The footsteps of her attacker in the kitchen are faint through the ringing in her head. She listens carefully, trying to make out what the man is doing and what his plan is next. There is no back door to her home, but the large window in the kitchen is plenty big enough for a grown man to fit through. She thought she could hear the window opening, but the sound was covered by the first voices from the officers on her front porch. The click from the circuit breaker, followed by the entire house going dark, add to her panic. She hears a few more footsteps in the kitchen and then the unmistakable sound of the window slamming shut.

The men standing outside her front door have no idea about what has gone on inside her house. They don't know that the killer has escaped through the back window. They don't know that she is waiting on the inside with an empty gun in her hand. They don't know there is a dead body in the entryway. They have no clue that they are about to walk into a very strategically planned trap.

6

The silence is scary. Tears flow from Jessica's eyes as she sits in her hallway in the darkness. The man who put her here is gone and she sits alone in her home, fearful for what is going to happen next. How did a night that started out so promising, with laughs and drinks over dinner, end up so frightening? She had no idea what the attacker was going to do when the red and blue spinning lights first entered through the crack in the curtains. The pieces to his escape plan started to fit into place quickly. From the best she can tell, the man has left through a window in the back of the house, having drawn the attention of the officers to the front door with the warning shots he fired into the door.

Her back is beginning to stiffen from the abnormal position it has been forced in to. She has tried to free herself from the colorful tape, failing at every attempt. She hadn't realized it at the time, but when the stranger taped her ankles to the leg of the chair, he also secured them to the legs of the table frame. This prevents Jessica from being able to stand up, her arms pinned to the top of the same table. Even with the gun secured in her hands with the tape, it shakes from side to side from her unsettled nerves. The weight of the metal causing the muscles on her forearms to burn, and the uncomfortable position of her back sending bolts of pain through her body.

The footsteps on the wooden porch break through the silence in loud bursts. The police begin shouting warnings to whomever is on the inside. Jessica tries but is unable to answer. They showed up to the house without knowing what was going on. Not long after they arrived, several shots were fired through the front door. This has the officers on edge and cause them to approach the door with weapons drawn. As the officers prepare to enter the front door, one lined up behind the other, they have no idea what they are walking in to and are prepared for anything.

Jessica can hear the soft whispers of the men, the silence inside the house only broken by their muffled voices and her heavy breathing through her nose. As she watches the door slowly begin to open, she tries to scream out through the confines of the tape. The officers enter the room with trepidation, opening the door without much conviction, their momentum halted as the door bumps against the dead body of Anthony on the floor. The beams of light from the officer's flashlights bounce from wall to wall, allowing Jessica to see the two men make eye contact with each other and hand gesture toward the body on the floor.

The sight of the dead man has made the officers tighten their grip on their guns further. Jessica is only a few feet away from them, but with the power out in the house, she has remained unseen. Her eyes dart from side to side, trying to follow the rays of light. She knows if the men see the gun in her hand first, they will act accordingly. Her only hope is that they see her face and body, and the predicament she is in, before firing their weapons. She has held her breath since the two men entered her home, fearing that any movement she made would startle them and cause an adverse reaction. A reaction that could prove fatal.

The officers slowly maneuver over the fallen body of the man Jessica was supposed to have dinner with this evening. The cops walk back to back, guns and lights swinging haphazardly around the living room. Every time the lights get close to her, Jessica whimpers to herself, certain that the end is coming. The officer closest to her turns slightly, allowing his light to travel from the floor, up the side of the table frame and stop on the gun in her hands. Jessica makes eye contact with the man and can see the fear in his eyes. The look of fear on his face both apparent and obvious. The sound of the man screaming the single word makes her jerk abruptly.

"Gun," the officer screams. His body reacting to the quick movement from the woman as if she was preparing to attack.

The room suddenly erupts in loud explosions, both officers firing their weapons toward the woman in the chair. Neither officer can see clearly through the darkness and smoke from their weapons. They fail to see the jerking of Jessica's body as the bullets rip through her flesh. When the shooting stops and the smoke clears, her body is bloody and lifeless, still resting in the unnatural position in the chair. The officers share a remorseful look before clearing the rest of the house.

When power is restored and the police investigators arrive, it was determined that seven shots had entered Jessica's body. The officers gave their statements, both telling the same story. They were called to the premises on a well-being check. Not long after they arrived, shots were fired in the home, causing them to fear that someone had been murdered inside. Upon entering the house, they found the body on the floor and not long after, the woman with the gun. There was no way the police officers knew the gun was empty, and they claimed to have fired in self-defense. The report from both officers was almost identical, even down to the fact that the only evidence of a struggle was the destruction of the bathroom door. They were able to explain this away by claiming that the woman must have trapped the man inside, and he was able to crash through the door to free himself. The officers were cleared of any wrongdoing, and the entire incident was officially listed as a homicide. There was no evidence found of a second man ever being in the home and Jessica was buried a few days later, forever branded a murderer.

ADULTING IS HARD

SUSAN'S STORY

1

The old Victorian house sits alone at the end of the street, surrounded by newly built cookie cutter homes. Tall trees and overgrown hedges cover the dilapidated structure in dark shadows, making the old house look like a single dead flower mixed in with the colorful bouquet of freshly built homes in the neighborhood. Most of the residents in the subdivision look down on the house as an eye-sore and wish it would just be torn down. Several residents in the neighborhood have circulated petitions to have the property condemned and the strict mothers strongly forbid their children from going anywhere near the place. Not everyone, however, looks at the rust-covered wrought iron railing around the front porch or the broken windows in the corner turret with distain. The current owner, for example, thinks the current condition of the home closely resembles the shambles she has created in her life.

Susan, like most kids, had lofty dreams and ambitious aspirations. Maybe it was the fact that her parents provided her with everything she could have wanted in life. Maybe it was the fact that she never took life seriously, no matter how turbulent the waves seem to be. Shortly after high school, Susan packed her bags and moved to Nashville. She thought it would be easy to write songs and become wildly famous, even if the only musical ability she had was playing a tambourine and flashing a smile. After two years of long nights in bars, abusive boyfriends and not being able to write a single hit, she packed her bags and moved back home.

Her parents were more than happy to welcome her back, her mom practically in tears with excitement. Susan herself gets a little teary-eyed as she thinks back on that day. Moving back into their house would mean she was admitting failure and that chasing her dreams was the wrong decision. Instead, with the help of her high school friend Robyn, she was able to work out a deal to buy this old house, and all its contents. The fact that the home came fully furnished was the final selling point considering when she left Nashville, Susan only had two bags of clothes, her boots and a fat little wiener dog named Fontaine.

For the first week, her days have been filled with countless hours of dusting, cleaning, scrubbing and making the dusty old place livable. It had been seven years since anyone had spent a night in the house, so all the furniture had the musty smell of old gym socks or clothes that had been left in the washer for a couple of days. She covered the broken windows with plastic sheeting and opened the rest of them to allow some of the cool breeze to air out the mustiness. Before falling asleep last night, she had made a list of things she wanted to accomplish this week, including going through the boxes in the basement and getting a handle on the landscaping in the back yard.

As she sits on the fancy regency sofa, a monstrosity that was meant more fore style than for comfort, feeding the crust of her pop-tart to Fontaine, all she wants to do is sleep. She has dreaded going into the basement. Even as a young girl she was not a fan of going downstairs in the house she lived in, which didn't nearly have the same eerie feeling of this old place. She looks down at her dog, who gives her an indifferent look, and swings her legs from the couch.

"I don't know what you're looking at me like that for. If I'm going down there, you're going down there."

As she nears the door to the basement, she can feel her heart race faster at just the thought of going down there. She had hoped to avoid the area altogether, but the curious side of her wants to know what's inside the dozens of boxes that cover the room. The wooden slats of the stairs creak under her weight and she nearly stumbles down the last few as Fontaine decides to weave himself between her ankles, a habit of his that has caused many a bruise to his owner. She manages to keep her balance by grabbing ahold of the not-so sturdy railing and doesn't even lose a drop of her coffee in doing so. The abundance of spider webs that she managed to plow through on her descent make her feel as if there are dozens of spiders crawling over her exposed skin. She does a quick pat and rub, trying to rid her body of the non-existent insects, before looking at the enormity of the basement.

The room is overwhelming. Boxes and large totes stand along the walls, stacked precariously high and nearly falling over. Old pieces of furniture are pretzeled together, covered in sheets and dust, and litter the space beneath the stairs. Electrical wires hang from the ceiling and run from one side of the room to the other. In the rare spots where the wall is visible through the clutter, pale pink insulation squeezes its way through. The light gray of the concrete floor is marred with small puddles surrounding the ancient water heater that sits in the corner of the room. Susan looks over everything, making mental notes of the dozens of repairs that will be needed down here.

She pulls an old dining room chair down from the pile and positions it next to the shortest stack of boxes. The cardboard nearly crumbles under her fingers and the contents fall onto the floor near her feet. Wilted and stained papers land silently all around her, but her attention is drawn to the large book that has remained inside the soiled cardboard. When she reaches in to grab it, the cold chills she has felt since coming down the steps, disappear. Susan rubs her fingers on the outside of the over-sized book, feeling the raised stitching and velvet material of the cover. The dark rose color is eye-catching when combined with the bright gold tassels that adorn the corners.

The object has piqued her interest and Susan doesn't hear the barking from the other side of the room. When the sound finally sinks in, she turns to shush the dog and sees that he is not by her feet at all. He is at the bottom of the stairs and focused on something at the top. After a moment or two, the dog quits barking and settles for a low rumble of a growl. This sound too fades after a moment or two, returning the basement to the eerie quiet. When Susan sits back down in the chair and begins to open the book, she is once again caught off-guard by a sound. This time, it's not the barking of a dog that startles her. It's the unmistakable sound of tiny feet running across the floor above her.

2

The tiny footsteps are followed by the sound of a small toddler laughing. Susan jumps from her seat, with the book clutched tightly in her hands. She stands at the bottom of the steps, looking up to see if whatever it is making the noises is going to show itself to her. Fontaine is frantically running in circles around her feet, anxious to be set free running toward the mysterious sounds. Susan gives him the hand signal he has been waiting for and he bolts up the stairs, his tiny little legs struggling to throw his portly body up the wooden steps. If she were not so terrified right now, Susan would laugh at the poor creature.

With the loss of her sidekick, the basement has returned to the damp, dark silence with which Susan initially found it. It gives her an uneasy feeling as she looks around the room, waiting to get the all clear sign from the dog. Her attention is drawn to the dark corner near the rusting water heater, the only part of the basement that is not fully illuminated by the single bulb that hangs from the ceiling. She works her way around the bottom of the stairs, holding tightly to the railing as if it would save her from anything dangerous lurking in the shadows. Her new vantage point allows her to see the tiny rocking chair that sits facing the wall a few feet from the heater. It looks innocent enough, obviously too small to be intended for use by anyone larger than a toddler.

As she nears the small wooden rocking chair, her embarrassment turns her cheeks flush red. She thinks that she must be going crazy for showing any kind of fear toward something so small and innocent looking. She turns around and heads back to the stairs, hoping to find her dog waiting for her at the top. When the rocking chairs begins to move on its own, she spins back around, and it abruptly stops. She had heard the soft sound of the curved leg moving back and forth, but she hadn't seen it. She stares at it, half wishing it would move again and half fearing that it would. After a few seconds, the scratching from Fontaine at the top of the steps draws her attention and she walks away from the rocking chair.

When she returns to the main floor of the house, she searches all the rooms and finds nothing out of the ordinary. There is no sign that anyone, especially a small child, had been running around while she was downstairs. She walks over and places the thick photo book on the stained Formica countertop before dropping her coffee mug in the sink. She had promised herself that she would make a dent in the work waiting for her in the basement, but that task will have to wait for another day. Instead, she decides she will sit in the backyard and go through the photo album. When she first moved in, several of her friends had brought her bottles of wine as a housewarming gift, a thoughtful gesture she is thankful for now as she grabs one and heads outside.

The landscaping in the back of the house is lush and severely overgrown. The hedges that surround the property act as a natural fence and block off the yards and streets in all directions. Susan had fallen in love with the yard, envisioning spending hours out here, sipping wine and working on writing music. The dog had followed her out the door and found a comfortable spot under the table to sleep, beneath the circular shadow cast down from the umbrella. Susan unscrews the cap from the top of the wine bottle and takes a big gulp. An added bonus to having so much privacy in the yard is that her neighbors will not be able to give her any funny looks for the uncouth way she drinks her wine.

She opens the album and scans through the first couple of pages. Nothing really catches her eyes as odd nor do any of the people in the pictures look familiar. She hadn't known any of the families who have lived in the house before her, so she's not really surprised. After flipping a few more pages, she comes across a large photo of a young boy. There's something about him that doesn't sit well in her mind. His pose is unnatural as he sits on a small rocking chair. His eyes appear to be open but not completely. The thought that the rocking chair could be the same one from the basement crosses her mind, but only for a fleeting second. She is more focused on the face of the boy.

Even in the dated picture, his face looks pale and lifeless. Susan slowly and carefully peels back the thin sheet of plastic film that protects the picture and removes the photo from the album. Upon further inspection, she is convinced that there is something not right about the way the boy was sitting. When she turns the photo over, she finds a name and a series of numbers. It doesn't take much thought for her to figure out the numbers coincide with the birth and death of the young boy. If the dates were accurate, which they surely were, young Thomas Bender had only lived to see his fourth birthday before he died.

Susan vaguely remembers reading a story on the internet a few years ago that went into detail about the burial process for children who died young. Some families would take photos of their children after death, many times propping the children up in lifelike poses. She wonders if that's what this picture is. If young Thomas Bender is already dead in this photo? She tosses the picture onto the patio table and takes a long swig from the wine bottle, finishing off the last of the fruity contents. She turns a few more pages in the photo album, trying to get the image of the pale boy out of her mind.

After a few moments, another thought absorbs her. Every picture in this album is taken from somewhere in or around this house. There are no pictures of the family members at the beach or on vacation. In every picture, they are either leaning against the ornate fireplace in the front room or captured standing near the railing of the spiral staircase that leads to the second floor. There are one or two shots of other kids, young teens from the looks of it, playing out here in the back yard. Susan removes a few of the pictures from the album and begins walking around the yard, trying to match up the scene in the picture with where the photo must have been taken.

The first photo is easy to compare. She looks at the picture and then turns back to face the house. The top of the turret that faces the front of the house can be seen in both the picture and the view from where she now stands. The house looks much better in the pictures than it does now but there is no mistaking that it's the same building. Her hands fan through the pictures, searching for another she pulled out that shows the back of the house. In this picture, there is a pretty lady standing in the window of the upstairs bedroom. Even with the poor camera technology that was available at the time the picture was taken, the woman is stunning. Her strong cheek bones are prominent and her flowing auburn hair curls down over her shoulder before coming to rest on the slope of her breast. In the photo, the woman has her left hand resting on a brilliant diamond necklace that hangs loosely from her neck and centers the narrow opening of her gown. The large diamond is bigger than anything Susan has ever seen.

Susan squints her eyes a little before holding the photo up in front of her face for comparison. She takes a few steps back to better frame the house to match the photo, and again raises it up to block the house from her view. She lowers the photo and is certain that the picture was taken in the exact spot she is standing. She goes through the exercise once more, this time holding the photo over the window for an exaggerated instance. She feels nostalgic as she looks at this house a hundred years ago, and then looks at it today with only a small movement of her arm. Confident that her assumptions have been validated, she lowers her arm and gives a passing glance at the second-floor window. The sun was in her eyes, but she would have sworn there was a woman looking down on her. She blinks quickly and looks again. There is no woman in the window, but Susan can see the glint from the diamond necklace as the mysterious woman runs away. The movement of the curtains assure her that someone had been standing in the upstairs window. Someone had been watching her.

7 Days in Hell

3

The pictures that were in her hands flutter to the ground as her trembling fingers release their grip. Susan walks to the shade of the patio umbrella, hoping that a few seconds of shade will help to clear her mind and figure out what she should do next. In a feeling of surrender, she drops down in the nearest chair and begins to sob. Buying this house was a big gamble, a risk her mother had warned her was not necessary. She wanted to be independent though, able to provide a life for herself that was hers and hers alone. This house was supposed to be the first step along the path of her becoming a responsible adult and a productive member of society. That dream world is starting to crumble and the pieces are staring at her from the upstairs window in the form of a woman she has never seen, except in a picture that was at least fifty years old.

If there is any hope of salvaging her new life, Susan must go upstairs and try to find the woman she saw in the window. She doesn't want to. Right now, she doesn't want to leave the warmth and isolation of the backyard. But there is no way she is going to call her mother and tell her she failed in another attempt to live on her own. And besides, the bottle of wine is empty and there is no chance she will last very long chasing ghosts or spirits or whatever it is lurking in the upstairs bedroom without more vino.

She grabs the empty bottle and motions to the dog to follow her inside. When she checks the fridge for more wine, she's disappointed to find that only the boxed wine she bought when she first stocked groceries is left. She didn't really like the boxed type, but when you're as budget strapped as she is, you buy what you can afford. There are no glasses or dishes in the house yet, so she fills a giant drive-thru soda cup with the boxed wine and drinks half of it before closing the refrigerator door. She refills the cup before heading to the foyer and climbing the stairs of the spiral staircase that lead to the upstairs bedroom and the window where she still swears she saw a mysterious woman standing.

Every step up makes her more nervous. She has climbed the stairs numerous times in the week since she moved in, but never when there was so much concern about what would be waiting at the top. The staircase itself can be intimidating, spiraling tightly as it covers the distance between the foyer on the ground floor to the turret on the upper floor. At the top, the round landing allows Susan to admire the view from the large windows that face the street in front of the house. The school kids have begun walking home, every group choosing to heed the warning of their parents by walking on the opposite side of the street to avoid the scary looking house.

The dark painted walls of the hallway blend perfectly with the cherry wood accents and trim, giving the corridor a warm and inviting tone. The room where the woman appeared in the window is the master suite at the end of the hall. Susan had not liked the room because it was so big. It made her feel even more lonely the first night in the house, so she had resorted to sleeping in one of the smaller guest bedrooms. The room she has been sleeping in is the first of the four doors in the corridor, and the only one with the door open, allowing the bright light from the sunshine to escape onto the worn carpet.

She rubs her hands along the wall as she walks, not because she needs to, but she loves to feel the grooves in the woodwork. The craftsmanship in the details of this home is something that newly built houses are lacking. She stands outside the door to the master suite, listening intently for any sound coming from the inside. The worn brass knob of the door sticks whenever it is turned, and the sound it makes as she tries to open it is so loud even Fontaine shudders. When the door swings open, Susan takes a giant step back. Her back is pressed against the wall on the opposite side of the hall, fearing that the unknown on the other side of the door is waiting to attack her.

When nothing happens, she takes a big gulp from the plastic cup and heads into the massive bedroom. The oversized bed sits against wall nearest the door and the remaining walls are covered with large oak dressers and a vanity. She has seen the furniture and bed before, so Susan doesn't even look toward these items as she walks to the window that faces the back of the property. She puts her wine down on the ledge and looks out on the area of the yard where she was standing a few moments earlier. She makes a mental note to go back outside and close the patio umbrella before bed to prevent it from being damaged. The long list of things she makes mental notes about has grown exponentially since becoming a homeowner.

Her nerves are beginning to settle a bit, helped along by a few more drinks from her cup. The view from this window allows her to see every inch of the rear of the property, including the small garden that sits past the row of tall hedges at the rear. She thinks it would be lovely if she were able to grow some fruits and vegetables back there. Her daydream is cut short by the loud clap of the door to the bedroom slamming shut. It startles her to the point that her hands swing wildly and knock her cup from the ledge, spilling its contents and leaving a large puddle on the hardwood floor.

She quickly gathers up the cup and puts it on the edge of the window, looking around the room frantically for something she can use to dry up the wet spot. She knew that old houses were drafty, so she just assumed a wind gust had come along and slammed the door. It isn't until she notices Fontaine growling at the door that she begins to get worried. She walks over to him and gives him a soft scratch behind his ears. Usually when she does this to him, he rolls over on his back and begs for his stomach to get equal attention. This time, his muscles refuse to loosen, and he continues to growl. She hadn't noticed the change in color and steam rising from the ornate knob on the inside of the door. When she reaches for it to open the door, it scalds the palm of her hand, sending her sprawling backwards and banging her head against the side of the large oak dresser.

4

Thump. Thump. Roll.

Thump. Thump. Roll.

The sound echoes through the room, seemingly on an endless loop. The pounding in her head seems to play right along with whatever the annoying sound is. When she opens her eyes, gone is the brightness of the sunshine that had filled the large bedroom with its warm glow. Now, everything is covered in gray, like a dense patch of fog had rolled into the room while she was knocked out. She is slow to regather her senses and it takes her several minutes to remember what had happened in the seconds before she passed out.

Thump. Thump. Roll.

Thump. Thump. Roll.

The sound is irritating and annoying, matching the pounding in her skull. Her dog is still by her side, but he has given up on his growling and menacing appearance, choosing to play the terrified puppy routine this time. Seeing the overweight canine is the first bit of normalcy that Susan gets. She has only been in the house for a week and only spent a couple of hours in this bedroom, so it all still feels like she woke up in someone else's house. She manages to gather enough strength to sit up and push her body against the wall under the window. She had forgotten about the monotonous sound until she heard it again.

Thump. Thump. Roll.

Thump. Thump. Roll.

The sound, whatever it is, is coming from the opposite side of the room, on the other side of the large four poster bed. Susan looks down at the dog, trying to persuade him to go over there and check out the source of the annoyance. In response, Fontaine shivers slightly and nudges himself in the small opening between the wall and his owner's back. She can feel the dog shaking, and curses herself for not getting a bigger, more fearless dog from the pound instead of this cowardly heap of fat. With a grunt and a groan, she manages to steady herself on shaky knees. The view out the window is different than it was when she first came in. It looks as if it's night, but the faint glow of sunlight can be seen in the neighboring yards. A dark cloud has planted roots directly above the house.

Thump. Thump. Roll.

Thump. Thump. Roll.

What in the world is that, she thinks to herself as she grasps the wall and inches herself around the corner of the bed? She jumps back in a startle when she first sees the young boy. He is sitting on the hardwood floor, his back resting against the rail of the bed frame, with his legs spread out in front of him. He stares straight ahead, trance-like, as he tosses a bright yellow rubber ball against the wall. She watches him for a few seconds, in shock, as he throws the ball again. It hits once against the wall, then bounces on the floor and rolls between the boy's legs.

Thump. Thump. Roll.

Thump. Thump. Roll.

His skin is pale and flaccid, the hollows of his eyes are bottomless orbs that have no life in them. She remembers back to the little boy in the picture, the one sitting on the same rocking chair she found in the basement. There is a definite resemblance there, but the poor quality of the old photo makes it hard to be certain. She steps back into the opposite corner of the room, hoping to gather her sanity in a safer location. There is no logical explanation as to who this boy is and why he is in her home. Is he one of the neighborhood kids who got lost and is as scared as she is right now? She guesses it's a possibility, but it wouldn't explain his appearance. The clothes he's wearing are old and outdated, and his skin is missing the colorization that comes from blood circulating through the veins.

Thump. Thump. Roll.

Thump. Thump. Roll.

The sobbing comes on without warning and the heavy breathing follows shortly after. She is alone, petrified, and out of answers. She knew becoming a responsible adult was going to be tough, but this is a little beyond what she had anticipated. She needs answers and the only place she will find them is on the other side of the bed, the side with the creepy boy and his damn rubber ball. She looks around the room, hoping to find something she can use as a weapon if needed. The large vanity and wooden dresser on her side of the room are completely empty and she curses herself for being too scared to sleep in this room. If she had, she would have unpacked her belongings in here and there would be dozens of things she could use to combat a small boy.

She scoops up the fat dog, straining as she does so, and holds him in front of her. There is no rhyme or reason to it, but she figures at the worst the dog will create a barrier between herself and the little boy. She will talk to the kid. She will ask him if he is lost and how he got in here. It all sounds so rational when she goes through it in her mind. Her quivering arms and wobbly legs have made it nearly impossible to form a clear stream of thought. She holds Fontaine in front of her as she walks, like the dog is a steaming pile of garbage that smells so bad that she doesn't want the fumes to invade her nasal passages.

When she turns the corner of the bed, the boy sits innocently on the floor, his eyes never moving from the wall. "Hi there," she says with no inclination of a response from the boy. "My name is Susan. What's yours?"

Her voice is trembling at nearly the same rate as her hands. The tiny legs of the dog are whipping about frantically through the air as if he is trying to run away and can't figure out why he is going nowhere. Susan stands firm, gaining more confidence with each uneventful second that passes. The dark cloud that is hovering over the house has now cast her shadow the length of the floor and covered the pale boy completely.

"Who are you and why are you here?" She raises her voice this time, hoping her change in tone will somehow produce a reaction. It does not. "I need you to get out of my house! I want you gone!" Susan is screaming now, the panic and fear raging through her body and exiting through her mouth.

The boy tosses the rubber ball once more.

Thump. Thump. Roll.

When the ball comes to rest between the boy's legs, he doesn't pick it up. Instead, he turns his head and looks at her. She can now see his entire face, when she could only see his profile earlier. The entire left side of his small head is a bloody mess of poorly sewn stitches and nasty scars. Where there was once his left eye, is now just a fleshy opening. The sight of his face sends rumbles through her stomach and she nearly passes out again. Fontaine lets out a timid yelp as the boy on the ground in front of them rolls his body over onto his hands and knees. He doesn't move quickly but when he completes the turn, he raises his head up to look at them.

His head doesn't move in a normal manner. Once their eyes meet, he keeps raising his head higher and higher, until the back of his skull is resting on his shoulder blades. His mouth swings wide, as if on hinges, and drops nearly to the floor. A surge of black, putrid smelling air, rushes from the open cavity and blows through Susan's hair. A high-pitched squeal, not that far off from a train horn, fills the silence. The onslaught of sounds and wind are almost unbearable, forcing Susan to wince and try to move her body away from the toddler.

With no idea what to do next, she tosses Fontaine toward the innocent looking boy who now resembles a four-legged zombie creature. She stands motionless long enough to watch as her dog hits the wood floor and slides across toward the evil thing. The moment his feet gather traction, Fontaine is hurdling himself away from the boy as fast as his little legs will take him. Susan follows suit and they both crash hard into the locked door on the other side of the room. She tries frantically to open it, even banging her body into it although she knows completely well that it opens to the inside. Without notice, the loud screeching stops. She looks down at the dog, he looks away in resentment. She thinks that maybe she had imagined the whole thing, until the sound of the rubber ball begins again.

Thump. Thump. Roll.

Thump. Thump. Roll.

5

The sound of the ball is constant and ominous. It shakes the walls of the old house with every bounce. Susan has given up on trying to open the door and stands defeated with her head against it. She pays little attention to the dog whining at her feet as she begins to cry loudly. All light is now absent from the room, even though it is still mid-afternoon. As she looks down at her burnt hand, a result from repeatedly trying to open the door using the knob that was glowing red with heat, it's hard for her to judge just how severe the burn is. The hand is throbbing, and she can feel the areas of skin beginning to bubble and blister.

She was so lost in her own pain and desperation that she had initially missed the exact moment that the sound of the rubber ball stopped. It was Fontaine nipping at the leg of her pants that brought her out of her self-loathing and back into the nightmare of this room. She turns slowly away from the door and her eyes are met by the warm blue eyes of the same lady she saw standing in the window from the back yard. There is a shadow of light that surrounds the stranger, making it appear as if she is glowing as she stands facing the little boy on the other side of the bed. Susan is far too worn out to react in any noticeable manner and simply tries to dry her eyes before the new lady can see her tears. She wants so badly to be a successful adult that she is unwilling to even allow a stranger to see her weakness.

She is hesitant, but Susan takes a couple of steps towards the woman. From the door she could only see the lady's back and the side of her face. She wants to make sure it is the same woman she saw in the window earlier and that the woman doesn't look familiar. As if feeling the danger from Susan, the glowing body turns abruptly. The speed of the movement causes the thin gown the woman is wearing to flow freely, like a flag in the wind. After seeing the woman's face, Susan is certain of two things. She has never seen her before, except in the old picture, and that it is also the same woman that was standing in the window earlier. Even in the pitch black, there is no mistaking the shiny necklace that hangs from the neck. The largest of the diamonds hangs loosely in her cleavage, glistening like a beacon in the dark.

She hadn't noticed it earlier, but while Susan had been mesmerized by the woman and the shiny necklace, the young boy has come out from behind the bed and is hugging the lady's leg. Shortly after seeing the boy standing there, Susan also sees the rest of the body of the woman. The lower half of her gown is blood stained and tattered. There is a giant hole in her midsection, allowing for parts of her intestines to hang loosely from the cavity. It takes everything she has for Susan to not throw up at the grotesque sight. When she looks away from the woman, she notices the back of the boy's head is also a collection of blood and gnarled flesh. Parts of his skull are missing and small specks of gray brain matter litter the sides of the wound.

These new revelations send Susan into a panic. She stumbles backwards, falling hard against the locked door with her eyes never leaving the pair on the other side of the room. So far, the two dead people have not made a menacing act toward her, but Susan wants to be as far away from them as she can when they do. There must be some reason these two have decided to show themselves to her, she thinks to herself in a rare moment of sanity. That second of clarity is quickly dismissed when the woman raises her right arm and points toward the door. She had expected fire or lasers to come shooting out of the woman's hand, but when nothing happens, Susan breathes a sigh of relief. The sound of the sigh almost made the slight click from the door go unheard. After a slight delay, her mind not putting together the pieces quickly enough, Susan spins and frantically tries to open the door again. This time, the knob does not burn her hand. Despite her nerves, and after several failed attempts, the knob turns and the door swings inward. Susan bends down to grab Fontaine, who hadn't realized the door was open for his escape and begins to move toward the hall.

The soft fuzziness of the plush carpeting on her feet feels refreshing in contrast to the cold hardwood of the bedroom. She gives a glance or two behind them to make sure the figures from the master bedroom had not followed them as she awkwardly heads to the end of the hall. Fontaine had been calm for the first few steps, but now he is frantic once more. Susan tries to console him and let the trembling dog know that everything is going to be alright, but her own lack of confidence makes it difficult. She stops in the hallway long enough to reposition the pooch in her arms, holding him tight to her chest. No matter what position she tries to put the dog into, he still manages to squirm and turn his neck toward the spiral staircase.

She was oblivious to the large man who was taking the stairs two at a time. When she spotted him as he approached the top, her body froze, giving Fontaine the opening he needed to escape from her arms. This man walks in perfect rhythm, neither racing nor meandering, as he clears the top step and turns to face her down the long corridor. From the best she can surmise, there are no bloody injuries to this new figure. The cloth of his well-tailored suit seems to be clean and free from blood stains. The only thing that makes him look peculiar at all is the color of his face, an alarming mix of blue and purple, and the odd angle with which his neck is bent. The man looks like he is trying to look under a bed, with his neck bent so sharply that his right ear is virtually resting on his shoulder.

Susan takes a step back every time the man moves toward her. His eyes seem to look right through her, as if he doesn't even see her. He has managed to back her into a corner, the only options remaining to her are to run straight toward him, or back into the room with the small boy and lady with the necklace. She opts for the latter and darts into the room, slamming the door behind her and using the weight of her tiny body to hold it closed. She stands in the same position for a long time, fearing that the man will push her over and barge into the room, and trying to avoid turning around and seeing the two dead people she knows already occupy this room. Just as she feared, when she turns around, she is met by the faces of the dead people, all three of them. She has no idea how the older man managed to get through the door, but he stands next to the woman and they all stare at her with desperate eyes. All color leaves her face as she realizes the predicament she is in. The color of her skin matches almost identically to that of the three people who are trying to kill her, a horrific shade of pale white death.

6

The three soulless bodies just stare at her. Susan doesn't speak and the eerie silence goes on and on, until the young boy breaks the silence with a menacing giggle. They stand in a row, the boy on the left and the man on the right, like the welcome party of a society of long dead ghosts. Each of them has a glowing aura that encompass their bodies, allowing enough light for Susan to see them all equally, and fear them all as well. Her eyes scan the room, looking for any sign of her dog, but she doesn't see him and hopes he was smart enough to get as far away from here as he could.

The large man is the first to move toward her. Her back is already to the door and she has nowhere else to go. She puts up her hands in a mock fighting stance, having never had to throw a single punch in all her life, and tries to put on her meanest face. She knows this will have no effect on the trio in front of her, but she doesn't know what else to do. The man continues to take small steps toward her, getting so close that she can begin to smell him. The thought of rotting meat comes to mind when she thinks about the odor. He stops a few feet from her and stares, his face locked in a crooked look of puzzlement.

"This is our house. What are you doing here?" The deepness of his voice seems to echo through vast emptiness of the large bedroom.

She hadn't expected him to say anything and the sound of his voice sends goosebumps down her body. His words were polite in nature, but the demonic sound his voice projected was so deep that it could have been summoned from the depths of hell.

"I bought it. I own this house now," Susan says, not really able to muster much more than a few terrified words.

"No," the man shouts. "My family built this house and we died in this house. It will be ours forever."

In an act of independence, her body decides to lower itself into the corner, cradling up like an infant in the crib. When he raised his voice and became angry, the color in the man's face turned even darker shades of blue. The skin on his face appeared to be flexing and bubbling with every labored breath he tried to take.

"Nobody but my family has ever lived here. We died in this place and we will see to it that nobody will ever live here again. So, get out of here you wench!" The two other figures have now moved closer and are standing near the man's back, the giggles from the small boy are the only thing that Susan can hear. The small child's voice penetrates her brain like a sharp dagger.

"I can't leave. I… I need this house." Even as she says them, the words sound like something a little girl would say. She thinks about trying to reason with the dead man, telling him that she needs to prove to her parents than she can be good at the adulting thing, but decides it would be ridiculous to try and reason with a person who died decades earlier. "You're already dead. Why don't you leave?" She regrets the words instantly, inciting the dead trio might not be the best idea, but her stubborn side decided now would be a good time to rear its ugly head.

The man doesn't respond to her verbally. Instead, he turns his entire body toward the two standing behind him. They both look up at him and the small boy begins to laugh louder. He also begins to skip around behind the others, chanting as he does so. "You're going to die. You're going to die."

His words echo as loud as the sound his rubber ball made earlier. Susan knows things just took a bad turn and she needs to do something. As the crooked neck man turns back to her slowly, she takes the opportunity to stand up and throw herself across the bed. She slides easily on the satin sheets, her body crashing to the floor on the other side. The first thing she sees when her body crashes to the floor is Fontaine, curled up in a ball and hiding under the bed. She doesn't reach for him or try to get him to come out, knowing in situations like this, its every creature for themselves.

She uses the side of the mattress to pull herself back to her feet. When she does, the large man is still standing on the other side of the bed, but the woman has positioned herself between Susan and the foot of the bed. They have her pinned down and trapped. The young boy, with the brain matter in his hair, is still skipping around the room and chanting. "You're going to die. You're going to die."

There is no time to ponder her options or think through what her escape plan should be. The crooked neck man has climbed on top of the bed and is crawling toward her while the woman with the necklace inches her way along the bed. If she didn't do something before they converged on her, the likelihood of her surviving would go out the window.

She thought these exact words, which gave her the idea for what she was going to do. The woman is by far the less intimidating of the two, so Susan elects to take her chances with her.

Just as the man on the bed reaches out to grab her, Susan takes off toward the woman with the necklace. She is hoping her momentum would be enough to overpower the entity. Their bodies collide in a thunderous crash, both women fighting desperately to maintain their balance. Susan can feel the heat from the woman, much hotter than what she felt from the doorknob. She can feel the strain on her body start to lower as her feet begin to gain traction, making progress in her attempt to get around the woman and escape.

She catches glimpses of things during the scuffle, not enough of them for her mind to recognize what they are and put them into context, just tiny screenshots of the things around her. The little boy skipping, the lady with the necklace reaching for her and the most important, Fontaine coming out from under the bed and placing his thick body at her feet. This last image is the one that sealed her fate. The dog was surely trying to help, but while she was struggling with the woman, he managed to stand in the worst possible place. Her foot struck his side and she was no longer able to keep her balance and began to fall.

It all happened in less than a second, but in her mind, it was a slow-motion series of events. Her body tumbling backward, her hands reaching helplessly for something to stop her fall, her back crashing through the glass of the large window. It was less than thirty feet from the patio below, and the fall itself would not have killed her. When her body landed on top of the sun umbrella, the sharp tip of the support pole impaling her through the chest, there was little chance at survival. Tiny fragments of glass continue to shower down on her face as she takes her last breaths. Her hands reach up to the sky, to where the three figures look down on her from the bedroom window. The dark cloud that had been covering the area directly above the old Victorian house suddenly dissipates, allowing the bright afternoon sunshine to return. The rays glisten magnificently from the large diamond necklace that hangs from Susan's limp hand as she exhales her final breath.

THE LONG FLIGHT

JAMIE'S STORY

1

It's days like today that make Jamie really hate his job. Everything was going fine until he got promoted and he found out the new position would require a weekly business trip. He would fly into a new city, handle about four hours of audits at the airport before spending the night in a hotel and flying home the next afternoon. This trip was going to be bad enough considering he was heading to his least favorite place, Newark, New Jersey. He had been dreading the trip all week, but he had decided it was only a couple of days. He had slept well the night before and woken with a positive attitude. It wasn't long before his outlook on the trip changed, caused by a series of random events that made his travel day become much longer than normal. He works in the airline business, so he knows there are things that happen that throw wrenches into a traveler's plans. It just seems like the whole toolbox was tossed at him today, and the feeling was overwhelming.

The day started out fine, with kisses to his wife and two daughters, before he loaded his car and headed to the airport. Once he hit the highway, the trouble began. What would usually only be about a fifteen-minute trip, turned into an hour journey. There was an over-turned truck that was blocking several lanes of the highway, making the already anxious morning drivers pretend they are the second coming of Jeff Gordon. When he finally made it to the short-term parking lot, he was in a serious race against the clock. He had only minutes to check-in and make it to his gate. The sprint to his terminal was hectic, especially for a man who stands head and shoulders above most other passengers. At six foot eight, his long legs hurled his body down the long hallway in record time. The airline personnel were all giggling when he made it to the desk and showed them his ticket, sweat dripping from his brow.

He was the last passenger to board the plane and to add to his already bad luck, he was assigned a middle seat. With legs as long as his, Jamie does not get comfortable on any flight. This particular flight, he has the misfortune of being squeezed between an overweight man who is already drooling in peaceful sleep, and a pregnant woman who looks like she is fearful that every breath she takes will be her last. He manages to secure his bag in the overhead compartment and squeeze his body into the seat. As his heartrate begins to slow from the frantic jaunt through the airport, Jamie begins to relax. He hadn't noticed the mechanics who climbed aboard and went straight into the cockpit area of the plane. When the announcement comes over the speaker system that there would be a delay, the chorus of unhappy moans from the cabin was thunderous.

The sleeping man on his right never stopped snoring for the entire hour that the plane sat at the loading gate. The flight attendant had to nudge the man awake when it was decided that the passengers would need to exit the plane. No details were given during that announcement, except to say that the airline was working on getting everyone rebooked on flights to their destinations. The pregnant woman, who had been nervous about flying, was now almost giddy with excitement to gain a few more minutes on the ground. The process of clearing the plane was chaotic, with people from the rear hoping to be the first ones off. There wasn't any pushing and it never came close to becoming a mob scene, but there were dozens of irate people looking to the flight attendants for answers. Jamie was a seasoned airline traveler, so he was on the phone with the person at his company responsible for booking his flights even before he got out of his seat. When he finally made his way off the plane, he was already booked on a flight that was leaving in about four hours. It wasn't an ideal solution, but his colleague assured him it was the best she could do.

Jamie had decided that with so much free time, he would break one of his cardinal rules of travel and have a beer and a meal in the restaurant. Even though he flies every week, Jamie knows that the food and drinks in airport restaurants are usually poor quality and over-priced. Robyn, the friendly bartender, takes his order and gives him the specials. He chooses the Szechuan Super Shrimp from the menu, breaking another rule he has, this one about eating seafood from a landlocked location, and orders a draft beer. The food wasn't bad, but the beer is even better. He spends about three hours exchanging messages with his wife, searching the internet and slowly sipping from his glass. The bartender keeps his drink full and the time passes quickly enough. The online surfing has diminished his cell phone battery and Jamie had intended to spend the last hour before his flight sitting near the gate and charging the device. When he searched for his charger, he realized it was another casualty of his hectic morning commute and the race to board the plane that wouldn't fly. There's no time for him to make it out to his car and get back through security in time for his new flight, so he decides to just wait it out and get a new charger when he makes it to New Jersey.

He is one of the first in line when the boarding begins, allowing himself ample time to get settled into his seat. He smiles slightly when he finds out his seat is in an exit row right next to the emergency door, complete with extra leg room. The plane only fills to about half capacity but the seat on the aisle of his row is occupied by a college-aged guy. Typical for a man of his age, the guy is apparently too involved in the music on his headphones to return the introductory smile that Jamie gives him. Once Jamie feels the doors close and the repetitive safety briefing from the crew begins, he leans his head against the window and closes his eyes. His day thus far has been filled with moments of panicked racing from one side of the airport to the other, followed by hours of sitting around and waiting for his new flight. The highs and lows of this crazy Wednesday, combined with the four beers he had at the restaurant, has left his body feeling exhausted.

He wakes from his deep sleep with the eerie feeling that he is being watched. He scans the nearby passengers and sinks back in his seat when he realizes nobody is paying him any unwanted attention. The night sky lets him know that he has been in the air longer than he would've guessed, and the rumbling in his stomach tells him that his body is starting to protest the seafood dish he had earlier. Before making the trip to the restroom in the back of the plane, Jamie gives another glance out the window. When he first sees it, out on the edge of the wing, he doesn't know what to make of it. It appears to be nothing more than a shadow. There are human-like features to the object, but the lines and bends of a human aren't there. It appears to be standing, with one arm outstretched and pointing at Jamie. He rubs his hand across the glass of the window, trying to get a better view of whatever it is out there on the wing of an airplane that is thirty thousand feet above the ground.

He rubs his eyes, hoping that fatigue, stress and the alcohol may be ganging up and playing tricks on his mind. When he looks again, the ominous figure is even closer to the side of the plane. He jumps, causing his not so friendly neighbor to give him an irritated look. He turns his attention to the passengers around him, wondering if anyone else is seeing the same thing as he is. He manages to sneak a peek at the older lady in the chair directly behind him. She is looking out the window but doesn't show the same stress on her face that he feels. She must not see the figure. If she did, she would be freaking out as much as he is. If she knew what Jamie did, that the shadow only shows itself when death is nearby, she would be hysterical.

2

When he turns his attention back to the vast darkness outside his window, Jamie is relieved to see nothing but the gray clouds. There is no more shadow figure. No more dark ghost. His stomach is still turning somersaults in revolt of the airport seafood and as he begins to get out of his seat, Jamie hears something that gives him a second or two of panic. It takes him a moment to figure out where the sound is coming from. When he sees the latch handle of the door to the plane move slightly, he practically jumps from his seat. His long legs take only a few strides to walk down the center aisle and once he closes the bathroom door, Jamie takes a deep breath and sits down on the toilet. He is sweating heavily, not believing what is happening. He takes several deep breaths and dries his perspiring palms on the leg of his pants.

Thinking back on the previous times in his life when he saw the same figure doesn't make him feel any better. His mind flashes back to a time when he was in the second grade. While he was daydreaming and staring out the window, the same figure appeared on the playground of the school. He had yelled in fright, which only brought the ire of his teacher who assured him there was nothing out there. The next day, his grandmother passed away from a massive heart attack. A few years later, while riding the bus home from school, he saw the same ominous figure standing on the sidewalk near his house. Jamie was afraid to leave the bus and he ran through his front yard as fast as his long legs would take him. When his mother saw him rush in, she thought someone was chasing him. When she checked, there was nothing there. There had been a few other times when Jamie was treated to an appearance from the same shadow, and every time, death was not far behind.

In the past, the image always appeared in the distance and was not that menacing. This time was different. This time, the thing appeared to be getting closer and pointing at him while it did. This is what has caused Jamie to rock back and forth on the stainless-steel seat of the toilet. A bathroom on an airplane is already a small place, but when you're well over six feet tall, the confined space becomes claustrophobic. He splashes some water on his face and tries to gather himself before returning to his seat, fearful for what he might find when he re-enters the cabin. A knock on the door hurries him along and he tosses the paper towel into the trash can and opens the door, giving the old lady from the row behind him his most apologetic smile.

He doesn't notice the other passengers on the plane, most of them sound asleep, as he makes his way back to his seat. His mind was focused on the windows that face the wing, trying to catch a glimpse of the shadow before returning to his seat. He stumbles and practically falls over as a young girl leaps from her chair and stands in front of him in the aisle. He feels like a giant next to the young girl, looking down at her startled. She smiles up at him, apparently oblivious to the speed at which the blood is rushing through his veins. The girl is blonde and pale, as if she has never seen the sunshine. When she opens her mouth to speak to him, her jaw swings wide, as if not attached to the rest of her face. The words come out deep and baritone, and cause Jamie to take a few steps back.

"Don't fall asleep!" the demonic voice says as it comes out of the mouth of this innocent looking girl, a girl that reminds him slightly of his youngest daughter. The girl says nothing else; she simply looks up at him with the same innocent smile with which she first looked at him. She steps aside and returns to her seat next to her sleeping mother. Jamie doesn't know what to think of the girl but given the thing that has been lingering outside of his window, she seems to be the lesser of two evils.

When he reaches his seat, the younger man on the aisle of his row doesn't even bother to move his legs to allow Jamie to slide past him. Once he is belted back in, Jamie reluctantly looks back out the window, fearful that the dark apparition would be floating just outside. There is no scary sight waiting for him in the night sky, only the low glow from whatever city lurks thousands of feet below. Confident that what he saw was a result of bad seafood and too much beer, Jamie closes his eyes once more, hoping to get a few more minutes of sleep before the plane lands in Newark.

He vaguely hears the lady get seated behind him, but he doesn't even turn his head to acknowledge her. The low hum of the jet engines help to drown out the static coming from the headphones of the man beside him and help to lull Jamie asleep. The extra leg room of the exit aisle allow him to stretch out his legs and get even more comfortable, a rarity for a man who is closer to seven foot tall than he is to six. He takes a last peak out the window and closes his eyes once more when there is still no sign of the menacing figure who haunted the night sky earlier. He leans his head back and allows the darkness of sleep to enter his mind, not noticing the cloud of darkness that has crept through the bottom of the plane door and has surrounded his sleeping body.

3

Jamie feels the vibrations through his body but doesn't open his eyes. He has been on enough flights to know that turbulence is common. When he feels the air rushing through his hair, hitting his face like a heavyweight punch, he jumps in a startle. He finds he is no longer strapped into the comfortable seat with the extra leg room. He can see the seat he fell asleep in, but now he is looking at it from outside the plane. Everything he sees is covered in a dark fog, like looking at everything through a blurry camera filter. When he realizes his predicament, his arms and legs begin to flail, looking for something, anything, he can find to hang on to. He manages to plant his palms on the cold metal of the wing of the plane, where he sits precariously. Panic fills his body. Even though the night air is freezing, sweat has covered his skin and completely soiled his shirt.

The dark figure appears once more, this time sliding down the side of the plane and nearing the wing where Jamie sits. It moves as if it has no bones, slithering and bending in ways a human form never could. It inches closer, and Jamie backs himself away. He finds himself getting further and further away from the cabin of the plane. He tries waving his arms as much as possible, hoping to get the attention of anyone looking out the window, but it has not helped his cause either. He can see that several of the passengers are awake and searching the night sky, but they either don't see him, or they can't see him. He feels lost and helpless.

Jamie looks back to the image coming toward him. The pulsating red lights on the wing of the plane help to illuminate it every few seconds. Each time he catches a glimpse of the thing, it is a few feet closer to him. When it gets close enough that Jamie can reach out and touch it, the relentless wind that had been beating at his exposed skin, suddenly stops. There is a calm that comes over Jamie's body, as if everything is now happening in a bubble and blocked off from the rushing winds around them. The shadow grows larger, surrounding his entire body. The change in the conditions have made Jamie confident enough to stand up completely. When he gets to his feet, he reaches his hand out to touch the shadow, his arm shaking as he does.

When his fingers first penetrate the edge of the figure, nothing appears to happen. He can't see the tips of his fingers, somehow they seem to disappear in the darkness. Moments later he feels the sharp pain. It races down his arm, through his chest, and tosses his body backwards. He lands in a thud on his back, staring up at the clear sky and bright stars. The body blow left Jamie feeling nauseous and he empties the last remnants of the airport food onto the cold metal of the wing. He wipes his mouth with his hand and when he does, he feels the pain in his fingers. His simple gold wedding band has melted slightly and became lodged in the skin of his ring finger. The edges of the ring are hidden below the reddened skin. In a state of shock, he rubs his ring finger with the opposite hand. Now with a new sense of fear, having felt the wrath of the violence the shadow is capable of, Jamie looks at the thing with more fear.

The apparition remains between Jamie and the cabin of the plane, blocking any chance for a safe return to his seat. The plane is still high above the clouds, making the lights below look like nothing more that twinkling stars. As Jamie once again rises to his feet, he can feel the shift in the plane that tells him the pilot has started the gradual decent. He looks over his shoulders and can make out the large cluster of lights that indicate the thriving metropolis that is Newark and nearby New York City. Relieved that he will soon be on solid land and hopeful that being so will end this nightmare, Jamie decides that avoiding the menacing spirit is his only option. Confined within the limited space of the wing will make the task almost impossible.

Avoiding the thing is easier said than done, however. The spirit moves quickly and without the limitations of the human body. It doesn't have the same fear of falling as Jamie does. It seems to hover, both above and below the wing where he now stands. His feet step back slowly, inching his way toward the tip of the wing. Jamie keeps checking the distance to the airport in front of him, hoping to be on the ground in the next few seconds. His body is still having to adjust to the uneven footing, the nose pointed down toward the ground causes him to lean his body to compensate for the angle. As the plane descends, every trip in and out of the clouds causes fear. The brief instances of not being able to see the thing in front of him leave him frantic. Once they have cleared the clouds, he can begin to make out the runways in front of them, the lights laying out a colorful geometric pattern below.

With no more clouds to block his view of the imposing shadow figure, Jamie can keep his focus on it. He watches as the edges of the shadow begin to retract. The edges pick up speed and seem to be collapsing on to each other, forming a tight round sphere. As it does, the gusts of wind that one would expect to feel when riding on the wing of a soaring plane return. Jamie nearly loses his balance when the strong wind tries to push his tall body in the opposite direction he had been leaning to compensate for the angle of the descent. The black circle of shadows now begins to shoot bright lights toward the sky, so bright that it causes Jamie to use his hand to shield his eyes. The thing now looks to be buzzing with electricity and power, gaining strength with every revolution it makes around itself. Even though the sky is clear above them, a low rumble of thunder can be heard over the roar of the jet engines. The grumbling becomes louder and louder, like a train you can hear coming from miles away and reaches a fever pitch as it roars all around him.

The pilot leans the plane slightly to the right. It forces Jamie to lean forward on his toes to stop from falling, keeping the cabin of the plane and the now circling orb in front of him. Out of nowhere, strong bolts of lightning begin to shower down on top of him. The first few miss him, but they slowly get closer until his entire body feels like it's on fire. The electricity surges through every inch of him, singeing the tiny hair on his arms and his eyebrows. The force pushes his body back and for a moment, his body lingers on the edge of the wing. He hangs there, as if holding on to an invisible rope. When the plane turns slightly to make its final approach to the runway, Jamie loses his balance and gravity takes over.

The plane was less than ten thousand feet above the ground when his body began falling. Jamie stared up at the airplane as it got further and further away. He didn't scream in terror nor did he try to fight against gravity's hold on him. He had a unique feeling of calm that ran over his body. He closed his eyes and thought of his wife and two daughters, and the pain they will feel when they hear the news. Even in his last moments alive, he mourns for his family. A single tear escapes his eye and is quickly brushed away by the force of the wind against his face. He opened his eyes shortly before his body came crashing down, just in time to see the dark shadow racing towards him like a missile. Where there was once no features to be seen, Jamie can now make out the horrifying details of a skeletal face. The bloodshot eyes, sunken deep into the sockets, are laser focused on their falling target. The remnants of exposed muscle seem stretched to their limits as the mouth begins to open, showing the last few rotting fangs the creature has left. The shadow picks up speed before piercing Jamie's body and disappearing through his chest, moments before they both crash to the ground.

4

Emergency personnel were waiting for the plane the minute it reached the gate. They rushed onto the airplane, evacuated the other passengers, who were oblivious that the tall man in the exit row had passed away mid-flight. The young guy who had been seated in the same row as Jamie was visibly shaken as he gave his story to airport police. He described how Jamie had seemed content until he walked to the back of the plane, presumably to use the restroom. The young passenger shows the officers how Jamie had violently thrashed about in his sleep, with arms and legs flailing. The college kid even went as far as to tell them it looked like Jamie was trying to hold on to the armrests of his chair, as if letting go would make him fall. He had thought the man was having a seizure or something similar, especially after he noticed the vomit and white foam that had formed around Jamie's mouth.

The flight attendants had attempted CPR and had even used the mobile defibrillator, both had zero impact on the fallen passenger. It was the medical staff that boarded the plane in Newark that made the official call and time of death was recorded. They wheeled his body off the plane and through the huddled passengers who were all required to give statements to airport police. The older woman who followed Jamie into the bathroom told them that when Jamie had left the room, there was a small odor of alcohol remaining. Another of the passengers informed them that they had seen the dead man at the airport restaurant before departure, and several of them had claimed Jamie was intoxicated. Every passenger who was on the flight had been identified and questioned about anything they saw regarding the dead man. All but the little girl. There was no record of any young children making the trip to Newark.

When his wife was told of her husband's passing, she was understandably upset. At first, the notifying authorities had simply told her they believed the cause of death was a heart attack. A few days later, following the autopsy, the official cause of death was changed to complications arising from a shellfish allergy. Jamie's wife fought this decision vehemently, knowing that shrimp and lobster were her husband's favorite things to eat. The coroner stood by his decision. After extensive reviews, the flight staff were also found to have done all they could. By the time they were notified that there was a problem, Jamie was already gone.

The authorities had tied the whole incident into a tight package, complete with a giant bow. They had dotted their I's and crossed their T's, all to keep the finger of blame from pointing at the airline. Jamie's wife, on the other hand, wanted answers. She refused to accept that her husband had a shellfish allergy, and that's what caused his body to shut down. She had the Health Inspector pay a visit to the restaurant at the airport, but the kitchen was judged to be immaculate. There had to be some other explanation. Jamie was healthy and rarely even complained of a sore throat or even a cold. She knew there had to be some other explanation, but she had exhausted all her options and had to let the mourning process begin.

A service was held for Jamie, which was attended by everyone who had ever met him. His wife was adamant that the service would include an open casket. As the mourners cycled into the funeral home, they stopped and gave her their condolences before making their way to the casket. Jamie looked peaceful in the coffin in his best suit, adorned with the tie he got for Father's Day from his daughters. Every person that stood next to coffin had the same thing on their mind, and their eyes went straight to the spot. They had all heard the rumors about his wedding ring, but until they saw it for themselves, they wouldn't believe it. The staff at the funeral home had tried to remove the gold band, but the only way to do it would have required the removing of his ring finger. Jamie's wife denied their request and the ring would remain soldered into his flesh for eternity.

When the mass of people finally leaves the funeral home, Jamie's wife is left alone with her dead husband. She talked to him, asking what in the world happened on that airplane. Her words echoed through the eerie silence and were only answered by her own thoughts. This is the first chance she has had to mourn for Jamie. He was her everything and now she is left in this cruel world to raise their two daughters alone. She breaks down in tears and sobs loudly while sitting in one of the folding chairs near the casket.

Suddenly, she has a feeling as if she was not alone in the viewing room and turns to see the body of a young girl standing in the dark corner of the room. It was hard to make out exactly who it was, but she assumed it was her youngest daughter. When the girl stepped out into the center of the room it was clear this girl did not belong here. Her skin was milk white and the rings around her eyes made it look like she had not slept for days. She is dressed in a blue dress and her blonde hair is pulled into pigtails. She holds a small toy plane, waving it through the air in a flying motion. The little girl stares straight at her, taking very small steps closer and closer without ever looking away. When the small girl opens her mouth to speak, the holes where there should have been teeth in her mouth began to ooze blood down the girl's face. Her voice came out slightly garbled and very deep.

"I told him not to fall asleep."

7 Days in Hell

THE DETOUR

JEANNIE'S STORY

7 Days in Hell

1

The restaurant has begun to fill up quickly, which is not unusual for a Saturday night. There are several booths along the wall, below the mounted swordfish, where groups of people are sampling from the same plate of appetizers. The voices booming from the bar seem to float above the crowd before mixing with the sounds of the music pouring from the house speakers and the sizzling from the fajitas, the latter being ushered to a nearby table with the aroma of the meat and peppers leading the way. Well-dressed restaurant staff scuttle about, weaving between tables in the choreographed dance that only seasoned restaurant staff can master.

In the center of the room, at a tiny table with only two chairs, Jeannie sits alone staring at the emptiness in front of her. The white tablecloth seemed innocuous enough when she was first seated, but after more than an hour, the only thing on the table is her seemingly endless glass of iced tea. Now, the brightness of the linen shines like a beacon telling the other patrons that Jeannie has been stood up. She knows none of the other diners of course, she only moved here about three months ago. In reality, the only people she has met in her time in this town are either coworkers or neighbors. Her time in the new city has been filled with disappointment; a job that was more stressful than she imagined, an apartment that was far smaller than she initially thought and a city that was not all together welcoming to a girl from the northeast.

Her inability to meet friends and the longing for a male companion led her to join one of the popular online dating sites, Friends First, mainly because the name sounded pleasant. When Jeannie first joined the site, she was instantly inundated with messages from men of all sorts. She knew this would happen, the reviews from these sites were crystal clear on the topic. What she didn't count on was the persistence of the men who were trying to meet her. Her mother always told her she was pretty, but don't all moms say those things. Most of the guys who sent her messages didn't even bother with small talk or asking her about herself. All they wanted to do was meet in person, probably for sex. Jeannie isn't a prude, but sex is not the first thing she thinks about when meeting a new man. She has an old heart. The type of heart that wants to be swept off her feet, wooed by a man, and treated like a lady.

Her mother had warned her about the troubles that could come from meeting men through the internet, but Jeannie chalked the warning up to an older woman being overprotective. The first man she met from Friends First was Mark. He was a nice enough guy, but the date was a disaster. Jeannie giggles to herself a little as she thinks back upon that date. What kind of man takes a girl to a sports bar on the first date, and on top of that, what kind of guy has his male friends at the bar waiting on him? There was no time for the two of them to talk, the loud hum of sports drowned her out every time she tried to say something. By the end of the night, which couldn't come fast enough in her opinion, Mark had turned his back on her, and she was literally searching the dating app on her phone while he ignored her.

It wasn't long after that dreadful date that Jeannie started talking to the man she is supposed to meet tonight. His name is Stephen and, according to his online profile, they have several things in common. He moved here from the northeast like she did, and he knows very few people in this town. If nothing else, she had hoped that tonight would go slightly better than her night with Mark, which ended with her closing the car door before he could lean over for a goodnight kiss. Jeannie and Stephen were both career-oriented, which would have been a good thing if it didn't make it that much harder to find a night they both were available to meet. Jeannie had plenty of work to do at home, but she also needed to get out of her cramped apartment. In her opinion, and the only one that really matters to a person living alone, tonight was the last chance to turn her luck around and embrace her new hometown.

Her mental exercise into how she got here is broken when the waitress asked if she needs more iced tea. She has already had more to drink in the last hour than she would in a normal day, so she declines. Jeannie is holding back the tears, the night becoming another in the long list of disappointments she has felt since moving here. Her parents had tried to prepare her for the troubles that come with moving your life to a new city, but Jeannie, like most recent college graduates, was ready to take on the world. That feeling has dissipated by the hour, one disappointment after another draining her of all ambition until finally, she is here tonight, spending her Saturday night alone and surrounded by dozens of others who are having a great time. The desperation is more than she can take any longer.

By now, every table is full of folks ready to enjoy a weekend night with friends. Jeannie checks her phone once more, hoping for a message from Stephen. Any message at all from him would make her feel better. Her phone is blank, except for the large digital display that shows she has now been sitting alone at this table for far too long. She leaves some cash on the table and exits the restaurant. As quietly and discreetly as possible, Jeannie manages to push her way through the patrons waiting at the front of the restaurant and out into a part of the city she is unfamiliar with. The fact is, the only parts of the city she knows are the immediate areas around her office and her apartment. Jeannie had taken a cab to the restaurant but as she scans up and down the busy street in front of her, there is no cab nearby.

Jeannie wants to get away from the restaurant, and the judgmental eyes of anyone who noticed her as she made her escape. She is surrounded by groups of people either coming or going, all smiley and boisterous. Jeannie keeps her head low in a manner to hide the disappointment in her eyes, there is no worse feeling than having complete strangers look at you with pity. She does her best to wiggle through the hoards, making her way to the corner after only a small struggle. She has never used the popular Uber app to find a ride home, but with no taxi in sight, tonight will have to be a first. The app downloads quickly and there is an available car practically around the corner from where she stands. After successfully navigating the correct online prompts on the phone to summon the car, she manages a sigh of relief, thankful that at least something went right for her this evening.

In a few seconds, a dark sedan rolls up to a stop in front of her and she climbs in. After polite greetings with the driver, a friendly enough looking older gentleman, Jeannie pulls out her phone once more and scrolls through her email messages that she had put off in favor of this dinner date. She debates on whether to send a message to Stephen to find out what happened to him tonight, but she doesn't want to know. Not right now while the pain and embarrassment of being stood up is fresh on her mind. She notices that her phone battery is almost drained, mostly from checking it repeatedly while she waited for her date, who decided to be a no-show. She curses the man under her breath and shoves the phone back into her purse before turning her attention to the now fading lights of downtown as the driver steers the car onto the highway.

Jeannie is hardly noticing the passing landmarks as the car cruises past, but once they hit the suspension bridge, she knows something isn't right. The bridge leads out of town to the south, and her apartment is about ten miles north of the city, this much she knows. She turns her head from side to side, trying to find anything that looks familiar. Her heart rate begins to increase as she sees the large buildings from downtown begin to shrink behind them. She turns to the driver, who keeps his eyes focused on the road in front of him and scoots her body to the edge of the back seat. Jeannie is a mild-mannered woman, her mother calls her timid, but her blood pressure is beginning to rise with each second they travel in the wrong direction.

"Excuse me sir, where we going? Do you have the right address?" Her normally soft voice comes out even softer, the fear grabbing ahold of her words.

"Yes ma'am. I know exactly where we are going," the driver says, a little too confidently.

"But I live in the other direction," she mutters.

"Yes ma'am, I know exactly where you live Jeannie."

2

At first, Jeannie is thrown back in the seat by the sound of her name coming from the mouth of the driver. She wonders to herself how he could know her name. The eyes of the driver stare back at her in the rear-view mirror, the dark brown pupils are intimidating, but he is hardly paying her any attention. She pulls her phone back from her purse and notices a message from Uber, the confirmation that her ride had arrived at the pick-up location. The power display is now blinking red, so she doesn't want to use the remaining battery life looking at the message, but one word catches her eye and causes her to click on the link. When the full message opens, her name is plastered in large letters at the top. She breathes a sigh of relief, thinking this explains how the driver knew her name. Of course the driver has access to her name. How else would he know he was picking up the right passenger?

Feeling easier, she starts to put her phone away, trying to save the little bit of power left on the thing, when she notices something else on the message. The photo of the driver and the vehicle that was supposed to pick her up, is nowhere close to the car she got in. She was scheduled to ride with a female driver named Robyn with a bright yellow compact car. It was dark outside when she got in, but she is almost certain that this car was black or a dark blue and this driver doesn't answer to Robyn. Her hands begin to shake, causing her to drop her phone onto the floorboard. She can see the light reflecting from below her feet, but she can't position her body in the right way to reach it.

She gives up trying to retrieve her phone and once again looks out the window, hoping to find anything that looks familiar that will tell her that they are heading toward her neighborhood. Gone are the signs of civilization that residents of a large city take for granted. There are no more strip malls or restaurants. The giant used car lots and sprawling hospitals are well behind them. The only thing she can see out the window is farmland and a few trees. She is now confident that the driver is not going in the right direction, but she tells herself to remain calm. Maybe he is just lost or maybe there is some reason he is taking this route.

"Sir, are you sure you're going the right way? This doesn't look familiar to me."

The man stares at her through the mirror, his face smiling and his head nodding. "Just relax. I know exactly where we are and where we're going."

It's not his words that put her mind at ease, but rather his face. He doesn't look like a person that would be capable of hurting her. The eyes of the man are warm and inviting, making him look like someone who would teach grade school or maybe be a pastor of a church. Other than his face and the back of his head, she hasn't seen much of the man. She can't see his prison tattoos or the scar on his face that runs from his chin to his chest. Jeannie once again returns her attention to her phone and grabs it with the first swipe of her hand. She presses every button on the thing, but it shows no sign of life. She shoves the dead phone into her purse as the car finally begins to exit the highway.

The entire off ramp is covered in flashing lights and orange barrels. Large metal signs point traffic to the detour route, which is a right turn at the stop sign.

"Is this detour the reason we went the wrong way from the restaurant?" Jeannie asks.

"Yeah, a detour." The driver doesn't look back at her when he says this, and with far less conviction than she would have thought he'd have.

Her hands are working overtime in the backseat, cracking her knuckles and biting her nails in a panicked dance. Jeannie is a smart woman, and no matter how much the driver wants to try to make her feel at ease, she is quickly realizing that something isn't right. She runs through the possibilities in her mind, starting with the fact that they have been driving away from the town for nearly fifteen minutes. She is confident that the detour on the off ramp played no part in the driver coming this way. She hasn't brought up to him the fact that the message she got on her phone told her that she was supposed to ride with a woman in a yellow car. She has never used the ride app before, so she isn't sure if it's common for there to be errors like that one. She's certain that there must be some bugs any time an app depends on the intelligence of the general public to be successful.

The inside of the car is now completely dark, matching the tone of the night and surrounding area. Jeannie can only see the road if she looks out the front window, where the headlights illuminate the dark pavement. She also notices that there has not been a single car drive by in the last several minutes. Being new to this city, she hadn't known that you could drive fifteen minutes in any direction away from downtown and be surrounded by absolute nothingness. She knew there were farms and large wooded areas around, she just hadn't expected them to be so close to the thriving metropolis. Jeannie decides it's time to speak to the driver once more, hoping to sound a little more authoritative, even though it's not in her nature.

"Sir, I know this is not the way to my apartment. I have already filed a complaint with Uber." This is a lie, but there's no way the driver can know this, so she feels no remorse about saying it. "I demand you take me to my apartment right now. I've already been in your car for over twenty minutes and I only live ten minutes from downtown."

The driver doesn't respond right away. When he does, the tone of his voice is completely different from the pleasant sound with which he spoke earlier. "Listen lady, you wanted a ride and got in my car. Now you want to tell me I'm doing my job wrong?"

Jeannie is first taken back, not expecting his change in tone and decibel level. She looks in the mirror and catches a glance at the man's eyes, which now seem ready to fire lasers. "I wasn't supposed to get in your car. The app sent me a message that said I was supposed to ride with a woman in a yellow car, but I didn't get the message until I was already in yours." She has lost the confidence with which she started this conversation, now just hopeful to hold back the tears that have started welling in her eyes.

"I don't care what the app told you, you're in my car now. I told you there was a detour."

"That detour is nowhere near my house," she says. "I just want to go home."

Again, there is silence for a few seconds, the only sounds heard are the sniffling from the backseat passenger and the low hum of the motor. "I told you I knew where I was going. Just sit back there and keep your mouth shut while I drive."

Jeannie doesn't know quite how to respond to this. Yes, the man has become angrier and more combative, two things she tries to avoid at all costs. He is also in the wrong and she is a paying customer, who should be treated with a little respect and receive the service she has paid for. She lets the sharp words fall silent and takes several deep breaths before turning her attention back to the driver.

"All I want to do is to go home. How much longer until we get to my apartment?"

The laughs from the driver cut through the silence like a dagger. His eyes fail to meet hers and his lack of a response infuriates the woman. She has not felt this much anger since she was a small girl.

She wrenches her hands together, causing her knuckles to turn white. She rights herself in the seat, trying to look as calm and professional as she can, hoping to calm the driver by looking a little less irate.

"I'm sure you know exactly where we are and where we are going, but I just want to know how much longer you expect it to be." Her voice has returned to the higher-pitched voice she uses while in the office.

"I'm not sure, the detour has backed everything up. Like I said, just sit there and let me do my job." The man doesn't even give her the courtesy of a look as he speaks.

This lack of respect flips a switch in Jeannie, and she refuses to sit here silently and let this man take her anywhere he wants. The fear that has begun to build up inside has caused her to become agitated, making her words come out sharp and loud.

"Tell me where we are and where we're going!" she proclaims. "I will never use this app again, mark my word."

"I'm sure the company will miss you, but you have bigger issues right now."

She doesn't really hear the words; her temperature is far above the boiling point.

"Take me to my apartment," she screams. "Take me home!"

This time the man looks back at her through the mirror, his eyes focused on hers. He can see the tears streaming down her cheeks that are flushed red with irritation. He flashes a small smile, showing the darkened and brittle few teeth that remain in his mouth.

"Jeannie, calm down. You moved here a few months ago and you hate this town. We both know that your apartment is not your home."

3

His words leave her breathless, but she stops herself from screaming and thrusts her body back in the seat, turning away from the mirror and his eyes. He knew she wasn't from around here and he knew she wasn't happy in her new town. There is no way for this man to know these things. This goes a little further than the information she provided when logging into the app earlier, they asked no questions about her past. The tears flow freely now, the realization that she may never make it home alive causing the salty dam to burst. The man continues to drive, turning a few times before pointing the car up a steep gravel driveway. Jeannie knows that whatever is going to happen to her, is only minutes away.

She searches the contents of her purse, hoping to find something she can use as a weapon. Much to her chagrin, she had only brought her smaller handbag tonight. There was only room for the essentials inside and unless she intends to stop an attack with a pack of tissues or a tube of lipstick, the things inside will do her no good. The speed the car is travelling has slowed considerably, and Jeannie searches the door for the handle, thinking that she could make a run for it once she felt comfortable the car has slowed enough to jump out without injury. Her hand touches the hard plastic of the door panel, but she keeps her eyes focused on the driver, not wanting him to catch wind of what she intends to do.

She moves her hand the entire length of the door before finding the small indentation for the handle. Her fingers move frantically and fail to find any way to open the thing. She is forced to remove her eyes from the driver long enough to look down and see there is nothing in the void of the door panel where the handle should be. Her eyes dart to the opposite door, and she can see this door is also missing the handle. The terror builds higher, the driver had evidently planned the events of this evening out in advance and her fate seems sealed. She tries to remain calm, but doesn't like the feeling of being trapped, especially in the back of a moving car driven by a stranger who obviously knows more about her than she wants him to.

The car comes to abrupt stop at the top of the incline, the momentum slamming Jeannie into the back of the front seat hard enough to force a small stream of blood from her nose. She reaches up and wipes the blood away, turning the frilly sleeve of her blouse an awful pink color. The man turns off the engine and swivels in his seat to look at his frightened passenger. He reaches his arm over the back of the seat and uses his thumb to wipe away another drop of blood from her chin. Jeannie tries to look away, but she is mesmerized by the man. His face looks innocent and grandfatherly, but his intentions seem to be anything but. Even now, she is wondering how this man can think of harming her when he was so soft and gentle when he reached back and rubbed her chin. Jeannie begins to think that maybe she is blowing everything out of proportion with her overactive imagination, an imagination her mother warned her would make life more difficult while living alone in a new city. The man takes his thumb, still covered in the blood from her nose, and sticks it in his mouth. Jeannie winces, and thinks that maybe she isn't taking it serious enough.

The man laughs loudly before turning around and exiting the vehicle, his baritone chuckle still resonating through her ears. Jeannie feels relief that the man has left her alone. Then she realizes, the man left her alone. She has no idea where she is and the area around the car is pitch black. She has no idea how long she will be here but a small part of her is hoping the man comes back sooner rather than later. She peers over the front seat, hoping to find a working phone or someway to get ahold of help, and notices the entire bench seat is covered in plastic. It seems odd to her but everything about this night so far has been odd. She watched the man exit the vehicle so there must be a handle to the driver's side door. Jeannie debates if there is enough energy in her panicked body to make a run for it if she were able to get out of the car. Considering the alternative, she decides that energy or not, there is no other choice. Jeannie slings the strap from her bag over her shoulder and begins trying to maneuver over the back of the front seat. There is little room between the top of the headrest and the roof of the car, meaning she will have to lay parallel to the ground and try to tumble to the front.

She begins by tossing her right leg over the passenger seat, trying to keep her eyes focused on the darkness beyond the window. When her foot comes down on the plastic covering the seat, she throws her body over and her left leg follows, crashing into the front console with a loud thud. Jeannie now lays on her back staring up at the roof of the car, listening for sounds coming from outside. Once she gathers herself slightly, she spins around and looks for the handle to the front door. Her hand feels around for the familiar metal object, something the body normally does without the mind having to tell it to. As she struggles to find it, fearing for the worse, the door opens, and the bright dome light of the car illuminates the lower legs and feet of the man standing outside.

The woman barely had time to scream before a thick hand smacks her across the face. His other hand entangles itself into her curly hair, forcefully dragging her body from the car. Her knees hit the hard dirt and pain shoots through her legs. Her body is writhing and shaking rather emphatically, her hands trying to grab at the man and scratch and claw his skin whenever she does. Breathing is getting harder and harder, her already tear-filled vision now becoming increasingly blurry. She can make out the car, her first prison, as it becomes smaller with every labored step the man makes. She is relieved when the movement stops and the man lets go of her hair, but she continues to scream. She rolls quickly on the ground once her body decides to listen to her brain, and watches as the man ties the end of a rope to a thick piece of lumber. She looks around and notices that she is in some sort of barn. The smell of old manure and animal urine hits her senses and almost causes her to vomit. The driver uses the other end of the rope to tie her feet to the same piece of wood, a thick post that is holding up the loft above.

Jeannie is a city girl, and never really cared for the outdoors or getting dirty. Now her body is covered in dirt and grime, her hair is a mess and she lost one shoe while she was being dragged across the ground. She yells obscenities to the driver, who ignores her as he walks out of the barn, the large wooden door slamming hard behind him. She is once again left alone, trapped inside this second prison. She tries to wiggle her legs free and has no luck, so she turns her attention to her surroundings. She has never been on the inside of a barn before, but if she had to imagine what one would look like, this would be it. Large wooden beams surround the place, each showing the wilting of years of work keeping the elements away from the prized livestock housed inside. The walls are covered in metal tools, large pliers, screwdrivers, and other instruments that she couldn't fathom a use for. Her eyes pass by the normal tools and settle on the row of handsaws. Starting at the bottom of the wall, the saws get larger in size as they go up, each meticulously attached to the wall and hanging innocently.

There doesn't seem to be any electricity in the barn, there are several lanterns scattered about the open space, giving off just enough light to allow Jeannie to see what's in front of her. There also seems to be more light coming from the loft area, the shadows dancing on the rafters above her. She can't see what's up there, but there have been no footsteps so she's pretty sure she's alone, which is how Jeannie prefers it right now. She begins sobbing, the desperation hitting her harder with each failed attempt to free herself. She tilts her head to look at her disarray, the missing shoe, her scuffed knees and her untucked blouse the obvious signs that the night has taken a wrong turn. The sound of the door slamming once more snaps her eyes back in that direction. She almost screams at the sight of the man who entered. Jeannie had expected to see the driver from the car. Instead, she is looking at the disfigured face of a new person, she assumes it's a man, but she could be wrong. His body is massive and covered in dark hair and his face is mangled and disproportioned. He's shirtless under a pair of denim overalls, his portly stomach pressing hard against the fabric. The skin on his face seems to twist slightly as the man sees her, apparently pleased with his newest prize. The muscles of his cheeks are stretched tight, scars creasing across his face where a nose would normally be. The monster had apparently been in some sort of accident involving fire, Jeannie thinks to herself.

He begins to walk toward her, rubbing his hands together as his body moves in a waddling motion. The new man doesn't attempt to speak as he moves past her and stands behind the pillar that's holding her up. Jeannie can feel his touch on her ankles as he loosens the knot and again as he holds her hair back to get a long whiff of her aroma. Feeling the skin of the grotesque man against hers gives her goosebumps and makes every hair on her body stand up. Once free from the rope, her body collapses to the ground. The man stands motionless, looking down on her. She scrambles away, trying to make her way to the door. With feet and arms flailing about, she manages to get a few feet of separation. When she nears the barn door, the loft area becomes clearer, and so is the alter of severed heads that is lit by candlelight.

She tries to move quicker, trying to convince herself that she can make it out of here alive. After seeing the half dozen or so skulls on the alter above this man, she knows these men intend to kill her. She grabs some dirt from the ground and tosses it towards the big man's face and at the same time, thrusts her shoulder into the door. It swings open wide, the fresh air hitting her face in a refreshing wave. Jeannie tries to climb to her feet, but her progress is stopped by the body of the driver, who stares down on her from above.

4

The driver meets her panic-filled eyes with a cold stare of his own, shoving her body back onto the floor. Jeannie tumbles and comes to rest near the feet of the ugly giant who had untied her. The big guy chuckles slightly, exposing the green and gnarled teeth in his mouth. When she sees them, Jeannie remembers her dad saying this is what you would call summer teeth, some are there, and some are not. She has no idea why this memory popped into her head at a time like this, but she quickly regains focus and tries to back away from the behemoth. He towers over her and looks far more intimidating than the driver, who is also moving toward her from the opposite side. She is stuck between them with nowhere to run.

"What's the matter Jeannie? Don't you like my brother Stephen?"

She doesn't respond to this, unless her sobs can be mistaken for a response. Jeannie continues to scoot herself along the dirt floor, using her hands as paddles to push her body further away from the two men. She tries to keep an eye on each of them at the same time, making her neck turn from side to side as if she were watching a tennis match.

"Why do you run, Jeannie? You are the one that suggested you and Stephen meet, now here we are."

Jeannie notices that the driver who brought her here is the only one of the two men to say anything. The larger man, Stephen apparently, only utters brief high-pitched grunts. They match strides as they move closer to her, confident that they have her cornered and have no need to rush. She has no idea what she is going to do to survive, but Jeannie knows her only chance to stay alive is to get away from these men. When the former driver slides a long knife from the sheath on his belt, the blade shimmering in the light from the lanterns, her mouth lets out a terrifying howl. The scream isn't the subdued sounds of kids on a roller coaster or in a haunted house. This scream has the ear curdling sound of a woman who knows she is going to die. In the movies, this sound would have been followed by clips of large flocks of birds leaving a tree all at once or innocent deer bolting across the field.

"You wanted to meet Stephen and I brought you here. I can't have you running away anymore. Stephen likes to play with pretty young girls like yourself." The man has made it close enough to her to reach for her leg. Her slight frame makes it easy for the smaller of the two, the driver, to wrap his entire hand around her ankle. She tries to kick free with her other leg but as she does, the giant grabs her and holds on tightly. "I guess we will have to make sure you can't run away anymore."

Stephen, the mountain of a man with the grotesque looking face, holds her by her calves and easily raises her body in the air. Jeannie is now upside down, staring at the knees of the two men. She can feel the blood rushing to her head, the tight grip on her calves becoming more painful by the second. She can't see anything the two men are going to do, but she can sense it's coming, much in the same way some people can feel the change in weather in their joints. Stephen is well over six feet, meaning that Jeannie can barely get her fingertips to the ground while she's being held like this, adding to the terror she feels.

With a swift swipe of the blade, the driver slices through the Achilles tendon on her left foot, in the area between the heel of her foot and her ankle. The pain is sharp and jagged, making her want to vomit right away. She feels a similar pain in her right foot, the one that was missing a shoe, as the knife slices though the ligament that stretches along the sole of her foot. What little bit of blood left in her feet now rains down on top of her, covering her face in the warm liquid before forming a puddle in the dirt. Jeannie is ready to pass out as her body is suddenly dropped and she comes crashing down on the dirt floor. Out of instinct, she looks down to her feet. Her left one has fallen at an impossible angle with the toes nearly touching her shin. The blood is beginning to return to its normal flow now that she is no longer upside-down, making the fluid gush from the wounds.

There is no breath left for screams. She can feel her body beginning to go into shock, the chills making their way along her arms. Stephen is now down by her feet, rubbing his hands in the puddle of her blood, covering his entire face with it. His grunts have turned to squeals, obviously excited by the site and taste of the liquid. Jeannie has given up any hope of getting out of here alive and just wants the nightmare to be over.

"Stephen, take up her to the loft and put her on the altar." Jeannie can hear these words even as she fights back the blurred vision, the ring of darkness beginning to squeeze out the light.

Her body is hoisted, and she closes her eyes. She can feel the sweat from the man as his arms carry her up the stairs. For a big man, he is extremely gentle when he handles her, placing her nearly limp body softly onto the wooden table that doubles as an altar. When Jeannie opens her eyes, she is met by the staring faces of six women, all without a body. This is the moment her body gives up and everything goes black.

7 Days in Hell

5

Jeannie struggles to open her eyes, not knowing how long she had been asleep. She remembers the two men, but at first, she thinks it may have been a bad dream. All she can see now is the large wooden beam on the top of the barn. When the droplets of water hit her face, she opens her eyes completely and turns her head to the side. The severed heads of the six women tell her right away that her memories were not a dream and she is still living this nightmare. She turns her neck to look the other way where it is greeted by more flying water. The driver is circling her body, flinging water from a brush he dips into an old metal bucket. The larger of the two men is standing idly in the corner, his monstrous face now covered with a black leather mask, but his overweight body is still wearing the same pair of denim overalls, now soaked in blood.

The men appear to be performing their own religious ritual, cleansing her body or something. The pain in her feet is excruciating, but she can see they have now been covered with rags to slow the bleeding. The pain is not her biggest concern. When she looks down, she notices that while she was asleep, the two men had stripped her of all her clothes. She lays on this wooden table, with her hands tied above her, wearing only a pair of lacy pink panties. The same pair of panties she bought this afternoon in anticipation of tonight ending in a much different way. Her modesty almost makes her nakedness become the most pressing concern and forces her to turn her head back to the six nameless faces.

These women must have experienced the same loneliness and torture that she is feeling right now. Some people say that you feel peace and tranquility when you pass away, but judging by the faces of these women, there is no way this is true. The skin is tight across their skulls and several shades of blue and purple. The eyes have all sunken deeply into the sockets, making each of the faces look like they were terrified in the last second before they died, which Jeannie thinks is a good bet. She can't take her eyes off these women, mesmerized by the looks on their faces. Most have mouths open, like they were killed in the middle of a scream. She doesn't want to end up like these women, placed on this altar and looking at the next woman who is unfortunate enough to meet these maniacs.

More pain hits her body. Not as brutal as the slicing of her feet, and this time it only lasts a second or two. She watches the big man, Stephen as he was called by the driver, circle her body and pour wax from the burning candle onto her naked chest. He doesn't touch her, nor does he make any sounds. She can feel the wax as it drips down the small mound of her breast and dries on her ribcage. She forces her eyes to follow him as he approaches her head on the opposite side, nearest the faces of the previous victims. Stephen stops when he reaches her neck and places the candle on the wooden table beside her. She can feel the heat from the flame, it's just hot enough to turn her pale skin pink. She looks up to the ceiling once more, closing her eyes and starting to say a prayer. Her time left alive is shrinking with every second, and she knows it.

Her prayer is broken by the moans and grunts of the big man. He must not be able to talk she thinks as she finishes her prayers and pictures her parents one last time in her mind.

"I know Stephen, but you know what happened the last time," the driver says.

More grunts and groans from Stephen. The driver looks at the big man, understanding the meaning of every sound, even though they all sound the same to the distressed prisoner.

"No, Stephen. Do I need to get you a mirror and show you what your face looks like? That is what happens when we let them live."

Stephen hangs his head slightly and returns his gaze to Jeannie and her bound body, apparently accepting the demands of his brother.

"Look brother, I know you like these girls, especially this one. Once we take care of business, you can do whatever it is you do with the rest of her body."

Jeannie tries to continue reciting her prayer to herself, tuning out the two men and trying not to think about what the monster has done to the bodies of the poor women who were captured before she was. Visions of her parents enter her mind, of being pushed on the swing in the backyard during the summer and building a snowman with them in the winter. The looks on her parent's faces as she drove away from the house a few months ago before beginning her new life, and the fear in their eyes. A fear that Jeannie also felt but refused to acknowledge. With her eyes closed, she sees her mother kneeling at the side of her bed and saying the nighttime prayers as she did so many times when Jeannie was younger, the two of them saying Amen in unison.

When the prayer is finished, she opens her eyes, hoping to see the loving face of her mother. When her mother isn't there, she lets out the loudest scream she has mustered all night. The yell goes on for seconds getting louder and louder, matched only by the joyous squeals from Stephen. The scream may have gone on longer, had it not been interrupted by the loud voice of the driver, the man responsible for bringing her to this place. The man responsible for sentencing her to death.

In a last moment of bravery, Jeannie turns to the driver and spits a stream of blood-filled saliva towards him. The spit falls harmlessly onto the breast of the man's shirt and doesn't even stop him from his undiscernible rumblings. His chants have turned from single words into a repetitive mantra, still in an unrecognizable language. The man appears to be in a trance, his eyes are rolled back, and he has appeared to have checked out, unaware of anything that is going on.

Jeannie turns her attention away from the driver, hoping to have better luck with the monster. The muscles of her neck are stiff and hard to move from side to side. She meets the eyes of Stephen at the exact moment that he begins to raise the large ax high above his enormous frame. He stops for an instance, allowing her eyes to look into his. For a second Jeannie thinks that there might be life in the man after all. She hopes that she can convince him with a look of sorrow and desperation to spare her life. Her plea has no effect on the man. The sides of his mouth begin to twitch into a grin as his hands start the long arc of the ax toward her throat. In the brief instance before the blade reaches her skin, she closes her eyes in a final rebellious act. She refuses to allow these men to see the fear on her face. She refuses to die like the others.

7 Days in Hell

7 Days in Hell

More books by Kevin M. Moehring

Sacrifice

The Twisted Timbers Series

Graham Park

Evil in the Woods

Town on Fire

7 Days in Hell

7 Days in Hell

7 Days in Hell

www.ingramcontent.com/pod-product-compliance
Lightning Source LLC
Chambersburg PA
CBHW071516110726
47908CB00003B/854